THE COWBOY

FROM

SIERRA BLANCA

A Western

R. Annan

One Vision Publishing

Chapter 1

One Saturday afternoon, a young cowboy, thirsty and dusty from traveling, walked into the Broken Bull Saloon in Denton, Texas, in the Nueces territory, and ordered a root beer soda. In spite of his young age of eighteen, he wore his gun in a professional manner, just below the hip and tied tight to the thigh. It was a single-action Army Colt in a plain holster, hardly noticeable in this land of many guns.

His order of a root beer soda got the attention of and a chuckle from four cowboys already lined up at the bar to his left. These four men, all from the big Circle L spread, took an immediate interest in the boy. They were the ramrod, Clint Mason, and his close partners, Tory Barns, Reb Jakes and Chubby Sparks.

Mason, wide of shoulder and six-foot-two, sidled over to the kid.

"Howdy, kid," Mason said. He smiled and looked down at the new arrival in a friendly way.

The kid looked up at Mason and returned the smile. He sized the big man up carefully for a moment, then said, "Howdy, mister."

Chubby Sparks, a short, robust, rosy-cheeked cowboy about the same age as the kid, came around to his right side and cleared his throat to get his attention. The kid gave him a blank stare.

"What's yer handle, friend?" Sparks demanded rudely.

"Jim," the young cowboy said indifferently, not liking Sparks' tone of voice or his stare.

"Jim what? Slim Jim?" Sparks replied with a snide chuckle.

"Blackwell. Jim Blackwell," the kid answered as he took a sip of his root beer and reached into the pickle jar. He had an air of confidence. His feathers weren't ruffled in the least bit.

"What's yer handle, lard bucket?" the young kid shot back at Sparks in a cool manner.

This quick reply set Chubby Sparks back on his heels. He suddenly realized the kid was no dumb sodbuster.

Tack, the barman, sensed trouble coming and decided to mellow things down. "Where ya headed, kid?" he asked.

"Just driftin'," Blackwell replied.

"Lookin' for a job?" Mason asked.

"Maybe."

The ramrod studied the boy's features. Curly, reddish-brown hair spilled out from under his wide-brimmed, dusty hat, and his freckled cheeks were colored a golden tan. His fine, clean-cut face was a face that would, without a doubt, attract women, especially the painted ladies. Blackwell had the look of innocence in a land of guns, sin and death.

The boy was a challenge. He was an open invitation for someone to try to remove that special bloom that comes only once in the life of a young boy or girl and then fades away forever, a one-time gift from nature.

"Did you say Blackwell, kid?" Reb Jakes asked, as if it were important but he couldn't remember why. The kid only nodded as he finished chewing the briny pickle. "Seems like I've heard that name before. You got relatives hereabout?"

"Nope," the kid replied.

He dug a two bit coin out of his jeans and put it on the bar, got a slice of beef jerky from a nearby jar and bit off a piece.

"So, yer lookin' fer work, huh, kid?" the ramrod asked.

"As I recall, I think I said maybe," Blackwell politely reminded him.

Tack, the barman, leaned closer and said, "There's a deputy job just opened. Pays twenty a month. You get three meals and a cot down in the jailhouse."

The kid considered that for a moment, then asked, "What happened to the last deputy?"

"Same as the last three. Lead poisoning," Chubby Sparks said, chuckling.

"And the marshal? Ya got a marshal, don't ya?" the kid asked the barman.

"Sure," Tory Barns replied, "if you can find him. He usually sleeps an' lets the deputy do all the work."

"Yeah," Blackwell noted with a wide grin. "I've seen thet kind before."

Reb Jakes jumped in with, "This bein' payday, the cowpokes will be comin' ta town, so he'll most likely ride over to Uvalde ta get outta the way."

Clint Mason studied the young cowboy for a moment and then said, "You never did answer me, kid. You lookin fer a job or not?"

"Ah," Reb Jakes said, "he looks like a cherry-boy ta me, boss. You ain't gonna hire no cherry-boy, are ya?"

The kid's eyes narrowed. He stared straight at Jakes. "I ain't no cherry-boy, mister," he growled. It was plain to see that he took offense at Jake's offhanded remark.

Reb Jakes, however, didn't seem to get the message. He looked at the kid for a moment then turned to his friend, Tory Barns. "Whatta you think, Barns? Is he a cherry-boy or not?"

Barns pretended to seriously look the kid up and down. "Naw, he ain't no cherry-boy, Reb. He's a momma's boy!"

All the Circle L cowboys burst out laughing, including the ramrod, Mason.

"I guess thet's why he's drinkin' soda pop instead of a man's drink," Jakes said tauntingly. "He's a greener."

The kid slowly turned to face Jakes. If looks could kill, Jakes would have been dead then and there. "You think I'm a greener, do ya, mister?"

"It looks like it ta me, sonny-boy." Jakes chuckled.

"Ya wanna go outside an' say thet, you polecat?"

The saloon suddenly went quiet. A challenge had been given. The kid had just braced a Circle L cowboy. Clint Mason looked at the young cowboy. He liked the kid's cut and the way he had about him. It was the bravery of youth he himself once had. The kid knew no fear.

"Don't say that, kid, unless you kin back it up," Mason said calmly. "Jakes is grease lightnin' on the draw."

"Well, he won't be when I'm finished with him!" the kid said boastfully.

Reb Jakes saw that he had gone too far. He smiled and put a hand on Blackwell's shoulder. "Have a drink on me, kid," Jakes said. "I was jest kiddin' is all."

The kid wouldn't buy it. "Stick yer drink up yer nose, mister," the kid growled. "We're goin' outside!"

There was a short silence. Finally, Clint Mason nodded, let out an exaggerated sigh and said, "Okay, let's go outside and get it over with then." He looked at the barman and winked knowingly. "Give me a can, Tack."

"What?" A look of confusion overcame Tack's face.

"The can. Remember the can?" Mason said, winking again.

The barman's face suddenly lit up. "Oh, sure! The can!" He reached under the bar and handed Clint Mason an empty number ten peach can. He kept several on hand to be used as spittoons for the poker games.

By this time the kid was already out the door. Mason, Barns, Jakes, Sparks and a crowd followed close behind. They all gathered on the street in front of the Broken Bull Saloon. Mason held the can up and addressed the young man.

"Kid," the ramrod said, "before ya start pumpin' lead, I want ya ta consider this." He looked at Jakes. "Ready, Jakes?"

Jakes nodded and stepped a few feet away from the others. Clint Mason grunted and gave the can a hard toss upward. It went spinning high into the air, sparkling in the sunlight.

Jake's hands moved fast as he slapped leather and fanned off five quick shots. The can danced, jerking left, right and up and down. Finally, it fell spinning to earth into an empty lot across the road from the saloon. An onlooker in the crowd ran over, got it and brought it back for inspection. It had five bullet holes in it.

Jakes reloaded his Colt, smirking confidently at the crowd.

"Did you see that, kid?" Mason asked.

The kid shrugged. "Sure, I saw it."

"Well, whatta ya think about it?"

"Not much," the kid said with a chuckle. "Heck, I know a one-eyed preacher who kin shoot better than thet."

No one spoke for a moment. This hadn't worked out as it usually did, with the cowboy jumping on his horse and riding out of town and nobody getting hurt. But the kid wasn't impressed. In fact, he was boldly scornful of Reb Jakes' skills.

"Then let's see what you kin do, kid," Jakes said defensively. "Sparks, go ahead an' toss up thet can agin."

"A double eagle is better," Blackwell said.

"What? Did you say double eagle?" Mason asked. "Yer jokin', ain't ya?"

"Nope, I ain't jokin'. I'm dead serious, mister."

They all looked at young Blackwell. Ramrod Clint Mason stared at the young man, trying to figure out if he was serious or just plain crazy. He couldn't tell for sure which one it was. There was only one way to find out, and that was to put the kid to the test.

Not taking his eyes off the kid, he pulled a double eagle from his jeans. He stared at it for a moment noting how small it seemed compared to the can. Finally, he looked over at the kid.

"You sure about this, kid?"

"Yup," Blackwell said calmly.

"How high?" Mason asked.

"As high as ya want."

Clint Mason nodded and swung his arm back and forth like a pendulum three times. On the third swing he sent the double eagle spinning. It sparkled in the sunlight as it arced upward. At some point gravity took hold and for a fraction of a second the coin seemed to rest in the air.

That's when the kid's gun barked and the coin disappeared.

The Circle L cowboys stood slack-jawed, staring up at where the coin should have been but wasn't anymore.

"Jesus!" Chubby Sparks said.

Tory Barns walked over to look around on the road. Finally, he stood scratching his head.

Chubby Sparks sniffed. "All I saw was a spark fly."

Reb Jakes said, "Christ! Who the hell are you kid?"

"I told ya, Jim Blackwell."

"Where are you from, Blackwell?" Mason asked.

"West of here," Blackwell replied. "Sierra Blanca."

"Jesus!" Jakes whispered in awe. "I thought I heard that name before. You're the Sierra Blanca Kid! You buttoned up Jesse Snyder in the Sierra Blanca County Range War, didn't ya?"

"That was last year," the kid said.

"Snyder's two pals is a-lookin' fer you, kid," Jakes said.

"Yeah, that's what I heard, too."

"Well, they'll never find you out here," Chubby Sparks said. "This is the end of the world. Nothing but scorpions and rattlesnakes in this place."

"Excuse me a minute, will ya, kid? I'd like ta palabra with my boys for a minute," Mason said.

"Sure," Blackwell replied. The small crowd stared at him from a distance, whispering amongst themselves and pointing at him. They had heard who he was.

The big ramrod took his men aside out of earshot to talk. "I like this kid," Mason said.

"He's got guts an' right now, with all the trouble we got at the Circle L, we could surely use another fast gun."

"I'm in," Sparks said. The rest nodded.

Suddenly Barns busted out laughing.

"What's so funny, Tory?" Mason asked.

"I was jest a-thinkin', boss," Barns replied. "What's gonna happen when the kid and ol' Lamont's granddaughter meet? She's gonna turn his head every way but loose! Haw!"

"Oh, Lordy," Jakes giggled. "I jest gotta be there when them two go head to head! She'll tighten his cinch, an' thet's fer sure!"

"Man, this is gonna be such fun," Sparks said, holding back a guffaw until his face almost turned purple.

Jakes predicted, "She'll chew him up an' spit him out!"

"Let's not mention her," Mason said. "It's gonna be like a mountain lion takin' down a rabbit! An' the kid's gonna be the rabbit!"

The kid stood looking on, wondering why they were laughing so hard. But it didn't matter. He was tired of drifting and was ready to come to roost. Anyplace would do, as long as it was peaceful!

Besides, he sorta liked these guys. He decided to hire on.

Chapter 2

It was early the following morning when they left the town of Denton. Clint Mason rode in the lead while the others came behind him strung out in a ragged column like lost sheep. Jim Blackwell was the last one in line and, like all the rest, was suffering from a head-throbbing hangover. He had switched from root beer to rotgut at the urging of the Circle L cowboys and now he sat on his big black mustang slumped over the apple and silently cursing every one of them.

It had been a night of drinking, dancing with the painted ladies and firing guns in the air until early Sunday morning. When the sun came up, it put an end to their fun. Mason collected his drunken cowboys and they rode away.

Many of the other Circle L men who had no weekend duties to perform had gotten pickled, too. Instead of suffering the long ride back to the ranch, they chose to stay in town at the cheaply-priced flea factory called the Hotel Moonstone or down at the stables. Others decided to sleep in alleyways because there was no charge.

Weekends were a cowboy's time to drink and howl at the moon.

For an hour they rode slowly across Circle L land, not seeing a ranch house or building of any kind. Fields of cholla cactus, bluestem and broom sedge stretched far into the distance, meeting up with towering banks of clouds on the horizon. Sometimes the riders passed small herds of cattle and cowboys slumped over in their saddles. Most likely they were dreaming of their girlfriends who anxiously awaited them back in town.

It was two hours before Blackwell saw a big, white, two-story clapboard house down in a shady draw with a barn, a corral, a windmill and a bunkhouse gathered close around it.

Clint Mason dropped back to see how the young cowboy was doing. "You okay, kid?"

"I'm a-dyin'," Blackwell muttered. His hat all but covered his face almost down to his chin, and his chin was almost touching his chest. "Somebody should shoot me in the head so I'll feel better."

Mason wanted to chuckle but was afraid his head would explode.

"How big is this place?" the kid asked, looking up.

"As big as the world, kid," Mason said. "Over twenty miles north, east, south and west, if thet means anything."

"Jesus. Who the hell is Lamont, God?"

"No, but then again, yes. He makes the rules here, kid. Break 'em and ya die. It takes an iron fist to keep things on balance around here."

"An' he's got it, I guess."

"You'll soon find out," Mason said. "You'll git ta meet ol' Nate Lamont face ta face, an' ya won't ever fergit it."

"What's he gonna do, bite my head off?"

"No, but he might talk it off."

"Yer kiddin'."

"Nope. The old man is proud of how he built the Circle L and he likes ta let people know it. But first he's gonna see if ya measure up ta his standards."

"Then it's him who does the hirin'?"

"Yep. I bring 'em in and he looks 'em over."

"What if he don't like what he sees?"

"Oh, he'll let ya know thet right off. He don't mess around."

Jim Blackwell groaned.

"What's wrong," the big ramrod asked, "gotta bellyache?"

"Christ," the kid said, "I got a darn hangover and now I gotta listen to a church sermon on top of it."

The others laughed. By now they were bunched up.

"Cheer up, kid," Jakes said. "The fun ain't started yet. Wait until we go chasin' down rustlers. You'll wish ya had never stopped fer thet soda pop back in Denton."

"Great," the kid moaned.

They all laughed at his misery.

Chapter 3

Because of Nathan Lamont's reputation, people expected to see a man as tall as a tree and broad as a river with eyes spouting fire and brimstone and teeth like pitchforks. Widower Nathan Lamont fell far short on all expectations. He was just a middle-aged man with prematurely white hair and a kind face. But he did have one thing, he could look into a man's eyes and see his soul. He could read his mind and tell what he was thinking.

At least that was the impression he left most people with.

During the Civil War, Nathan Lamont was a rancher near Beaumont, Texas. He made big money smuggling horses, cattle and guns across the Mississippi River to the Confederate forces.

From 1861 until 1863, business was good but abruptly came to a halt when Union gunboats took control of that great river. Finally, the Union blockading of Texas ports spelled an end to Lamont's thriving enterprise.

Things got worse when the war ended and the South was overrun by carpetbaggers and Union businessmen who worked to reconstruct the South in a different image. Politics especially got nasty. The effects of reconstruction were soon felt in every part of Texas.

But Lamont, being a savvy businessman, had an ace up his sleeve. The eastern states had been left with a scarcity of meat. The war had demanded food for millions of soldiers on both sides of the Mason-Dixon Line.

Virginia, Delaware, New Jersey and Massachusetts were sucked dry by the demands of the war, as was Florida, one of the largest producers of beef since the 1840s.

Then came the great discovery. In the vast, dry, hilly, cactus-covered area called the Nueces, Spanish cattle that had drifted across the Rio Grande to the Sabine River had been free to multiply unmolested for over a century. There were now literally millions of cattle roaming free, on their own, waiting for the hands of man. Some said the cattle had actually been there as early as 1690. Since Texas was now part of the Union, these cattle were now on Union land and belonged to Texans.

When Lamont heard of the growing interest in the cattle of the Nueces, he decided to take a chance. He sold his ranch in Beaumont and moved lock, stock and barrel southwest into the Nueces badlands, a place where only the strong survived and where millions of Spanish longhorns were free for the taking.

With his twenty loyal cowboys, Lamont staked out a twenty-square mile perimeter between the area that was later to be known as Carrizo Springs and Eagle Pass. The land was dry and harsh, but the cattle there were sturdy, though long-legged and stringy. They were clearly not meant for dairy use but for meat. It took some years of interbreeding with Herefords and Devon heifers, shipped in from Kentucky and eastern states, to produce an animal suited for eastern dinner tables.

But there were problems. People on both sides of the border saw what Nathan Lamont had and they decided to take what they wanted without paying. Cutting off large pieces of his herds and rebranding them, they sold them in Mexico and northeast Texas.

Law enforcement in the Nueces didn't exist. Small bands of outlaw Mexican vaqueros drove Circle L cattle across the Rio Grande into Mexico and got two or three dollars a head with no questions asked. Renegade cowboy rustlers took bigger chunks and headed them north to the cattle towns where they were able to sell them for as much as five to ten dollars a head. Cows were going for twenty dollars at the St. Louis stockyards.

To combat this problem, Lamont separated his men into two groups. The largest group of twenty cowhands was made up of regular cowboys whose job was to tend to the herds, including roundups, trail drives, breaking horses and other jobs. They worked under an assistant ramrod. A small, elite group, called trackers, worked under Clint Mason. Their special mission was to catch rustlers. The trackers were hand-picked by Mason. So far the group was made up of Tory Barns, Reb Jakes and Chubby Sparks, as well as Mason.

So, on Sunday morning, while Nate Lamont was sitting in his rocker on the front porch of his ranch house getting some fresh air, his ramrod Clint Mason came riding slowly into the yard with a new man. The man's bent over posture raised Lamont's curiosity.

"Had a good time in town, Mason?" Lamont asked.

"Yes, sir," Mason replied, "real fine, sir." He, Barns, Jakes and Chubby Sparks slowly dismounted. Jim Blackwell sat slumped over his saddle horn, snoring loudly.

"What have you there, Mr. Mason? It appears to be a young cowboy sleeping in his saddle."

"Ah, I found him in town, sir. Thought he might be worth taking a look at."

Just then, assistant ramrod Fred Saddler and three of his men, Yancey Newman, Dipsey Parnell and Tuck Gamble, came riding in. They saluted Mr. Lamont and headed towards the corral. One of them, Dipsey Parnell, had fastened his eyes on the sleeping cowboy as they went by him. Halfway to the corral he stopped and turned his horse around to have a closer look.

Suddenly he dismounted and shouted. "Jim Blackwell, ya rotten polecat!"

Parnell's loud yell shocked the kid awake. Startled, he jerked upright and fell backwards over the cantle. He did a complete somersault, flipping heels-over-head, and landing squat on his duff on the ground behind the mustang.

Everyone who saw it broke out laughing, except Mr. Lamont. He stared in wonder as the young man grabbed the horse by the tail and pulled himself up, first to his knees and then to his feet.

Jim Blackwell looked around in a dazed fog for his hat only to find his horse had one hind foot in it. He was about to bend down to get it when Parnell shouted again from down the yard.

"Draw, you skunk!"

Clint Mason, Barns, Jakes and Sparks looked first at the kid, then down at Parnell.

"What's the matter?" Mason asked, stepping between Blackwell and Parnell.

"Step aside, Mason," Parnell growled, "thet sidewinder kilt my pard, Sam Turner, back in Sierra Blanca a year ago! I been hopin' ta run into him someday!"

All this time Jim Blackwell was trying to move his horse's foot off his hat. He met with little luck. The big black mustang stubbornly refused to budge.

Mason turned to the kid. "Is thet right, kid?"

"Heck, I don't know. I kilt half a dozen of them bushwhackin' sidewinders. They was all hired guns." The kid grunted as he pushed hard on the horse's rump.

"Well, you better take care of business, kid," Mason said. "You kin worry about the hat later."

Just then the animal snorted and stepped off the hat. The kid slowly picked it up, dusted it off and slapped it on his head. He checked his Colt and stepped out into the middle of the yard to face Parnell.

Mr. Lamont shook his head. This kid was going to be dead even before he got a chance to talk to him. He called down to Parnell. "Hold up a minute, Parnell. Is this really necessary?"

"I'm afraid it is, Mr. Lamont, sir. I promised my pard if'n I ever got a chance I'd take care of this."

"Maybe it was your friend's time to go," Mr. Lamont replied. "Can't you put it to rest, son?"

"I'd like to, Mr. Lamont, but I can't break my promise."

Lamont sighed, "Alright, if you must."

Parnell looked up at Jim Blackwell. The kid stood loose, his arms down by his sides. "I'm gonna holler and ya better draw, kid," Parnell barked loudly.

"Don't do it, Parnell," the kid said. "I beat Turner fair an' square. You know thet."

"Draw!"

Parnell went for his gun. Before he even got it halfway out he was looking down the barrel of the kid's Colt. Parnell's face turned deathly pale. He knew he was dead. He stood and waited for Blackwell to shoot.

Nate Lamont got up from his rocker and walked down into the yard. He looked at Jim Blackwell. "Put it away, young man," he said softly.

As the kid put his gun back in its holster, Lamont motioned to the two young cowboys to come to him. When they were close, he put a hand on each one's shoulder.

"Boys," he said, glancing at them both, "the past is the past. Nobody can change that or bring the dead back to life, except God. Now is the time for living." He waited a moment, then looked into Parnell's eyes. "You came within one second of meeting your maker. This boy did the decent thing. Will you give him that, Parnell?"

Parnell nodded and sighed. He reached out and shook Jim Blackwell's hand.

"Thanks, Parnell," Blackwell said.

"I'll have yer back from now on, Blackwell," Parnell said.

"An' I'll have yers, too, Parnell. Thet's a promise."

Lamont nodded and smiled. He knew now that Clint Mason had brought him a good man and a fast gun. And he needed plenty of fast guns.

Chapter 4

Theft of cattle by Mexican rustlers was the least of Nathan Lamont's worries. By conservative estimates, he and the smaller ranchers were losing over 50,000 head of cattle a year to local outlaws.

With no law for protection, the ranchers suffered rape and torture at the hands of outlaws of the worst kind. Homes were being burned to the ground, and defenseless people were shot and hung. Trails were unsafe. Stagecoaches were ambushed on long stretches of road that led from town to town.

The thieves that Nathan Lamont hated the worst were the ones that took the animal's hides and left the carcasses rotting in the sun. These criminals killed the cattle, skinned them and tossed their hides on a wagon. Sometimes they didn't even bother to make sure the animal was dead. Using a special knife, they hamstrung the cows, hit them in the head with a sledgehammer and went to work removing the hides as fast as they could. Sometimes while the calves stood by watching and bawling in fear. They even killed the calves and took their hides, too.

Collecting cow hides was a lucrative business that brought as much money as cows did at market. The hides made their way as far east as Europe to supply the tanning business, a multi-million-dollar enterprise for the making of everything from furniture to hats.

These were the men Nathan Lamont despised the most. At least a rustler had some respect for one of God's most precious creations. Not so the hide-peelers.

Again and again hundreds of dead, bare carcasses were found in the remote areas of the Circle L. They were easy to find. All one had to do was look up into the sky. Wherever those big, black, long-winged, red-necked vultures rode the winds aloft, dead cattle were sure to be found below.

Sometimes the stench of death rode the winds. The horses were always the first to pick it up. They would start fidgeting nervously, their eyes bulging at the smell of rotting flesh. One glance skyward told the cowboys where the carnage was to be found.

Those carrion-loving scavengers pointed the way. All the cowboys had to do was follow.

To combat this problem, Lamont put together a small team of fast-riding, sure-shooting men. These men were not your usual cowboys. They were loyal to the brand and would follow orders. And those orders were to stop the hide-peelers. Any hide-peeler caught was hung. It was harsh justice, but it was the only kind of justice available to the ranchers, and it took a tough cowboy to handle a job like that.

Ramrod Clint Mason's trackers were housed in a separate bunkhouse a few yards from the regular one. This is how Lamont wanted it and it gave them a special status at the Circle L. They also enjoyed higher pay than a regular cowhand.

"Are you sure about Blackwell?" Lamont asked Mason a day after meeting Blackwell.

"I'll give him a try and see how it goes, if ya don't mind, sir," Mason replied.

"He might not like what he sees out there. Some don't."

"Then we'll know," Mason said. "If he can't stand it, then you can give him to Saddler."

Lamont nodded. "Alright. If he doesn't measure up, I'll put him in with the other cowboys riding herd."

After that, nothing more was said about Jim Blackwell.

Lamont thought of his little select group as his lawmen, which is basically what they were. They would ride out and search the skies for the birds to tell them where the hide-peelers had struck last, then track them down and give them Nueces justice by hanging them. It took a special kind of man who could stomach that kind of work day after day. Knowing it was not an easy job, Lamont paid the trackers double cowboy wages.

Apprehending the hide-peelers required special skills and coordination. Mason and his men had to act as a unit. Each man had to do his part without hesitating or waiting for instructions. The hard part was getting to the fresh kills so they could follow the wheel ruts made by the heavily-loaded wagons. A wagon carrying fifty hides made deep grooves in the earth and was easy to track.

One day, after three days out, they got lucky. They were out on the fringes of the herd when, one morning after sunrise, they saw the vultures circling above a ridge about five miles away. Packing up quickly, they rode out, not bothering to have breakfast.

Mason urged his mount into a gut-busting run. Like a starved wolf on the scent, he hunched forward in the saddle and let the wind whistle past his ears. Two miles on he gave his mustang its head and held tight.

When they got to the kill site they found the carcasses were still fresh. The buzzards had just begun to drop down for the feast. When the cowboys rode in, those ebony soldiers of Satan scattered to nearby scrub oaks and stared at the intruders in silence.

A single calf stood bawling by its dead mother. Three other calves lay skinned nearby. One was still alive. The trackers dismounted. The kid watched as Mason and the others walked amongst the carcasses looking for the suffering, the ones not yet dead. They shot them in the head, including the calves.

The kid stood stone-faced, clenching his fists, staring at the cruel devastation scattered about him. Suddenly the smell was too much and he bent over and heaved.

"The kid's got the quivers," Barns chuckled.

"He'll git used to it," Jakes said.

Mason walked over to Blackwell and put a hand on his shoulder. "You wanna ride back kid? It's okay if you do."

The kid shook his head. "No, I don't wanna go back. I wanna get them varmints, is what I want." He got his canteen and rinsed his mouth out.

"Let's go, men," Mason said. They mounted up.

The hide-peelers had two wagons, and their wheels cut deep into the earth under the heavy weight of their cargo. It made them easy to track.

"They're about an hour ahead," Chubby Sparks said.

"They're headed for Uvalde," Barns offered.

"Think they heard all the noise we made?" Jakes asked.

"Maybe, maybe not. Depends on the wind," Mason replied. A second later he said, "Nevertheless, let's be alert. If they heard us, they'll most likely set up an ambush."

It was late in the afternoon when they came to the top of a rise and stopped to look down. They saw the hide-peelers below. They had two wagons piled high with hides. Each wagon had a driver and a man with a rifle on the bench. Four riders with rifles rode one on each side of the wagons.

The outriders kept looking around, front, side and back. Suddenly one of them yelled and they spread out into the nearby gullies alongside the road. In a moment they had disappeared from sight.

"They're on to us," Barns said.

"If we ride in to stop the wagons, they'll ambush us," Jakes added.

"Slick move on their part," Sparks said.

Mason nodded. "They're sure smart, but I know their game." He twisted in his saddle and looked over at Jakes. "It's yer move, Reb. Make it fast."

Jakes eased his slim body down to the ground and grabbed his special Winchester with a scope on it from its sheath. Bending low, he sprinted down the rise to a clump of scrub oak and bushes thirty feet away. He stopped just as a rifle barked and kicked up dirt nearby.

"They saw ya," Sparks yelled down to Jakes.

"Find out who's doin' the shootin'," Mason said.

They all got their rifles and took up firing positions on the edge of the rise, staring down at the wagons. The wagons were still moving.

Suddenly two more shots came in Jakes' direction.

"I see the rascal," Jakes shouted. Without waiting, he levered off a shot into a cluster of cactus to the left of the wagons. They heard the unmistakable bone-crushing thud of the bullet on flesh. There was a groan and a return shot went wild.

"Good shot, Jakes!" Mason hollered down the slope. "You drilled 'em!"

Suddenly rifles barked from below and bullets kicked up dirt on the rise by Mason and his men.

"Roll back, boys," Mason yelled and they all scrambled down below the line of fire.

"Kid," Mason said, "tie the horses further down."

Blackwell scrambled to his feet, grabbed the horses' reins and tied them to a scrub oak in a shallow gully twenty feet back. He quickly returned and lay on the ground next to Mason.

"Watch Jakes, kid," the ramrod said.

Jakes, lying on his belly, levered off two shots, and the two men on the first wagon went spinning to the ground. Two more shots followed and the other two drivers flipped over the sides. The driverless wagons slowed to a stop.

Jakes quickly scrambled to the left, taking cover in a new spot, just as the outriders below shot at where he had been a second before.

"Five down, three more to go," Mason said.

Suddenly one of the outriders yelled up to them. "Hey, you up there! Let's make a deal!"

Mason waited a moment then yelled back, "What kind of a deal?"

"You guys git half the hides."

Jakes whispered up from below, "Keep 'em talkin', boss."

Mason nodded, then yelled back to the outrider, "Is that the deal?"

"It's fair, ain't it? Hell, we did all the skinnin' fer ya!"

"I guess so," Mason replied, "but the thing is, yer all dead men."

"What?"

Jakes' Winchester barked again. They heard it hit the outrider where he crouched behind a patch of ground juniper. He fell forward into view.

Suddenly, two horsemen went pounding down the road as the remaining two hide-peelers rode off.

"Go git 'em, men!" Mason screamed.

Barnes, Sparks and the kid sprinted down the back side of the rise to the gully where the horses were. Jim Blackwell was the first there and, before the others were even in the saddle, he was riding hell bent for leather up over the rise. His big black mustang went skidding down past Jakes who gave out a rebel yell and waved him on.

By the time Barns and Sparks rode down the rise, the kid was past the wagons and out of sight.

"Jesus!" Jakes yelled up to Mason. "Look at thet kid go!"

Mason had a worried look on his face. Maybe the kid was biting off more than he could chew.

The two hide-peelers had a good head start but the kid's big mustang had better wind. The quarter horses soon began to tire. The kid's tall, lean body let the wind slide past as he leaned in over the apple. His hat soon went sailing behind.

Half an hour into the chase, the kid was within range. He pulled his Colt, took aim, and carefully thumbed off a shot at the nearest rider. His bullet took the fleeing man in the back and knocked him out of the saddle. He went crashing into a cluster of cactus.

The kid never looked back. His mustang shot past the dead man's horse and towards the last rider. The man, in desperation, turned and thumbed off two shots. One bullet cut a piece of flesh from the kid's left shoulder. He flinched and fired a return shot, hitting the hide-peeler in the back of the head. The man's body jerked crazily as he tumbled onto the road.

The kid pulled his mustang to a halt. He sat panting like a dog and took a drink from his canteen. He poured water on his wound. Barnes rode up first, then Sparks came with the kid's hat.

"Thanks," Blackwell said, putting his hat on. He suddenly realized how tired and hot he was.

Barns looked at his arm. "Yer winged, kid."

"I'm fine," Blackwell replied.

"Jesus," Sparks said, "but you sure are one hard-ridin', fast-shootin' fool, kid!"

"I guess I'll take thet as a compliment, Sparks."

"I meant it as one." They rode back to join Jakes and Mason.

Chapter 5

The smoke rose high into the air like a twisting, turning black snake, standing out vividly against the pure blueness of the afternoon sky. The cowboys stood watching the wagons and hides burn along with the piles of dry brush they had stacked beneath and around them. Satisfied that the fire was going well, Mason called for his men to mount up.

"There's a stream ten miles back," he said. "We'll camp there for the night."

"Whatta we gonna do with the bodies?" Blackwell asked.

"We'll do the same fer them as they'd have done fer us," Mason said. "Let the buzzards an' the coyotes fight over 'em."

They tied the outlaws' horses and the wagon horses on a long rope and started off with them following behind like a caravan. In little over an hour, they made camp and ate by a stream in a cluster of scrub oaks. They were hungry, as it was the only meal they had eaten so far that day. Later they dropped their saddles and rolls and made their beds close to the fire. By then it was dark and had gotten cold.

"How come we didn't bring Mr. Lamont the hides?" Blackwell asked Mason.

"He wouldn't touch 'em, kid," the ramrod said.

"How come?"

Barns asked, "Say, kid, how long you been around cows?"

"Not much. I mostly broke broncs. Had a lot of other jobs, too, like ridin' shotgun fer a stage line, but I'm mostly a bronc buster."

"Well, kid," Jakes said, "I noticed one of them hides looked a lot like ol' Sally, a cross-eyed heifer I knew. She was a cute little bugger and tried ta dump me every chance she got. I kinda fell in love with the little rascal."

"You ever been on a trail drive, kid?" Sparks asked.

"No, can't say as I have. What's thet got ta do with anything, Sparks?"

"If ya go on a trail drive, you'll understand, kid."

"How so?"

"Well, when you leave the herd at the stockyard ta be taken by rail to St. Louis, it suddenly hits ya that ridin' back without them cows sure is a sad thing."

"Cowboys don't go to St. Louis if they don't have to," Mason said. "It stinks of dead cows. Cowboys don't like the smell of dead cows, kid."

"Why?" Blackwell asked.

"Thet's where they do worse to them cows than the hide-peelers do. It'll turn yer stomach an' you'll never get the stink of blood outta yer system no matter how ya try."

Blackwell didn't understand but said no more.

They were three days out and by the time they rode into the yard of the Circle L they were caked with dust and stunk like wet skunks. They took care of all the horses, including the outlaws' mounts, and turned the saddles, saddlebags, rifles, gunbelts, guns and harnesses over to Mr. Lamont, plus the four hundred dollars they had taken off the bodies.

"It all belongs ta the boss fer his losses," Mason said.

There was an outside shower on the west side of the bunkhouse. It had a large, open-top oak cask set on top of a trestle. The cask held fifty gallons of water. It was usually filled by hand by carrying buckets of water up from the water trough next to the windmill. A ladder led up to the cask. A five-man line, using five buckets, could fill the cask quickly. A canvass tarp with an opening formed a rectangular enclosure to provide privacy.

It was a convenience hardly any cowboy used unless ordered to do so by their bunkhouse buddies when their body odor became too ripe to tolerate. The Circle L cowboys preferred the fast-running stream half a mile away where there was plenty of privacy.

Young Jim Blackwell, however, made good use of the portable shower the same day he returned from the range. On a table in the enclosure were soft cotton towels and cakes of lye soap, a soap strong enough to peel paint off of wood. The scent of the soap penetrated the skin and clung for days. It was believed to keep mosquitoes and chiggers at a distance for months. For some reason painted ladies like it, which was one of those mysteries as yet not revealed to mankind.

It was while young Blackwell was occupied with scrubbing the grit and grime of the trail from his body that he heard loud voices coming from the house. It seemed that two people were in a shouting match. One voice clearly belonged to Lamont, but the other one didn't. In fact, when the tones of the other voice fell on the kid's ears, he stopped scrubbing his skin raw and stood listening in wonder.

No, it couldn't be, but, yes, it was. The other voice was that of a young girl. It would never be mistaken for the voice of Viola, Lamont's cook, washer-woman and house cleaner. This voice rang like a delicate bell, even in its anger.

The arguing went on between Nate Lamont and this other person. The sweet, sing-song, bird-like sounds of the girl's voice contrasted with the deep, husky voice of the man.

Suddenly it stopped. A door opened and slammed shut. Blackwell came out from behind the canvas curtain that enclosed the shower. He saw the flash of coal-black hair and fair flesh on the porch as someone leaped down and shot across the yard like a bolt from the blue.

As the kid buckled on his gunbelt, his eyes followed the figure's movements. It ran down to the water trough to where he had left his big mustang to rest and drink. He wanted it rested up before riding into town with the boys to dance with the painted ladies. For a moment the figure paused to look around.

It was then that Blackwell realized it was a young girl!

She saw Blackwell but ignored him. Grabbing the mustang's reins, she vaulted up into the saddle and tried to get it moving.

Blackwell was later to learn that the girl was Alice Fuller, Lamont's granddaughter. It seems Nate Lamont had sent his daughter, Mary, east for an upscale education after his wife, Judith, had died. While there she married a lawyer named Frank Fuller. Alice was their only child, a spoiled, college-educated, headstrong brat.

Alice Fuller was doing her best get the mustang moving, but all it did was stand still and snort back at her. It also stared across the yard at Blackwell as if to say, "Who the heck is this, boss?"

This allowed Blackwell a perfect view of the black-haired, blue-eyed beauty.

She was dressed in one of those fancy eastern riding get-ups he'd seen in magazines. She wore those tight pants called jodhpurs and a linen shirt with a red and black checkered design. The vest was tanned leather as were the high, smoothly polished boots. On her head was a flat, black crowned hat like those worn by Spanish bullfighters.

She was sitting on his horse in his saddle, and she looked just fine.

But it was those big, blue eyes and pouting red lips that made the kid stand slack-jawed and still as a love-struck school boy with a silly grin on his face.

Jim Blackwell had never seen the likes of Miss Alice Fuller in all his days on earth. He smiled at her and this seemed to make her angrier than she already was.

"What are you gawking at, you idiot?"

Because the phrase came from such a perfect mouth, all Jim Blackwell heard were velvet tones and poetic words.

Since he just stood there with a stupid grin on his freshly polished face, too petrified to talk, she came at him again. "Well, fool? Has the cat got your tongue?"

The best Blackwell could do was stand dumb as a rock and grin. His ears were turning pink.

Alice Fuller glanced up at the porch where her grandfather now stood smiling. "Is this an example of one of your finer hands, Grandfather?"

Lamont chuckled and nodded. "Why, yes. He's one of my best, Alice, dear."

The girl glared at Blackwell. "Well, tell him to move on. He offends me with that stupid grin of his."

"I'm afraid you're on his horse, my dear."

Suddenly realizing who the fool really was, Alice Fuller thought quickly. She cleared her throat and replied, "Well, I thought everything belonged to you, Grandfather. All the cows and the horses, too."

"Not all the horses, dear. Most of them, yes, but not all of them."

Alice stared hard at Blackwell. "What's his name, Grandfather?"

"Who, the horse or the cowboy?"

"The cowboy."

"His name is Blackwell. Jim Blackwell." Lamont chuckled. "And don't you hurt him."

Alice Fuller stared at Blackwell as if seeing him more clearly now that she had a name for him. It slowly occurred to her that he was a handsome young cowboy about her age. He resembled one of those drawings in the romantic western magazines she had read on occasion. Only better.

She took special note of his reddish-auburn hair and freckled face. He had the look of freshness about him, like a new pair of boots. A bit of wildness sparkled in his eyes. She liked the special way he wore his gun.

"Is he the one you told me about, the crazy one who rode recklessly into the mouth of death to kill those hide-peelers?"

"That's him, dear," Lamont replied. "Would you like a formal introduction?"

"No, I can take care of that," Alice Fuller said as she glided smoothly from the saddle and walked over to stand about a foot away from Blackwell. She stepped back another foot as the antiseptic smell of the lye soap hit her.

Her own personal expensive perfume took a bite out of his senses, too, and he wanted to get closer but was too afraid to move.

She held up a gloved hand to be kissed, saying, "I'm Alice Fuller. Mr. Lamont is my grandfather."

Blackwell stared cross-eyed at the glove, not knowing what she was expecting. She saw his confusion and lowered her hand. This was too much to expect from a simple cowboy, anyway.

Suddenly he got up courage and blurted out, "I'm Jim Blackwell an' I jest took a bath, Miss Fuller, ma'am!"

A roar of laughter came from the porch and the bunkhouse. Even Viola laughed when she heard that one. She was hanging out clothes alongside the house.

Alice Fuller ignored the laughter and said, "What's wrong with your horse, Mr. Blackwell? He won't do as I tell him."

"I'll have ta talk ta him about that, ma'am," Blackwell said. More laughter came from nearby.

The young cowboy walked quickly over to the mustang and put a hand on its neck. Alice Fuller came up close and watched as Blackwell whispered into the horse's ear.

"What did you tell him?" she asked when Blackwell was finished.

"I told him he was a darn fool if he didn't take a pretty girl like you fer a walk."

For the first time, Alice Fuller showed the cowboy a little respect. She smiled at him and said, "I see. You talk to horses, do you?"

"Only to Blackie, ma'am. Me an' him understand each other pretty darn well."

Blackwell took the girl's hand and placed it on the mustang's neck, then stepped away.

"Tell him how good-lookin' he is, ma'am," the cowboy said.

For a moment Alice Fuller smiled. Then she nodded and said, "You really are a handsome fellow."

The horse snorted, shook its head and turned its gaze upon her. It pressed its warm muzzle against her shoulder.

"You wanna take her on a date, ol' pal?"

The horse shook its head and whinnied loudly.

"Kneel," Blackwell said.

The horse neighed again and slowly got down on its front knees and waited.

"He's all yers, ma'am," Blackwell said.

Alice Fuller grabbed the reins and climbed cautiously into the saddle. The horse waited until she was settled and rose up. She gave him a boot-tap on the barrel and turned him.

The big mustang moved through the yard gate at a gentle trot. Alice Fuller now had a chance to put her riding lessons from school to good use. She tapped his barrel harder and off he shot like an arrow from a bow, heading for a far field across the way. Those in the yard saw her grow smaller and smaller until she eventually became nothing but a tiny dot on the horizon.

A half hour went by and Cliff Mason told Reb Jakes to go look for her. Just as he was about to mount up, horse and rider came pounding across the field. She was soon back at the water trough in the yard.

"Grandfather, I want this horse!" she cried out.

Lamont looked down into the yard at the young cowboy. He motioned for him to come up on the porch.

"Look," he said softly so no one else could hear, "She's only going to be here a short time. A week or two, at most. Just as a special favor to me, son."

Blackwell nodded. "Sure. But he's plumb tuckered out right now. He needs a proper brushin' down, some grain and a good day's rest. Thet bush grass didn't do him much good."

"Alright. You show her how. It's best that she learns it's not all about jumping into the saddle and riding around, anyway."

The kid nodded and walked back to Alice.

"I heard what my grandfather said, Mr. Blackwell." Alice dismounted. "I've been to riding school back East. I know how to properly groom a horse. He won't complain when I'm finished with him." She paused a moment. "I won't need your saddle and gear. I have my own."

The girl took the reins and led the horse down to the barn. Blackwell followed. Once there, the cowboy tossed his saddle and gear on a stall fence and watched as the girl fed and brushed the big mustang down. He seemed to be enjoying the gentler touch.

When she was finished, she put him in the corral and walked over to Blackwell. She said, "I apologize for being so rude to you, Blackwell."

"Jim. Jim is better."

"Alright, Jim." She stared at the young man and looked puzzled. "You're called the Sierra Blanca Kid, aren't you?"

Blackwell glanced down at his feet and blushed. "Who told you that, ma'am?"

"My grandfather. He talked a lot about you."

"He did? I don't know why. I ain't nothin' special."

"To him you are. All of you are."

Blackwell decided to change the subject. "About Blackie, ma'am?"

"Yes?"

"Keep him in the corral when yer not a-ridin' him. He likes the company of other horses."

"Alright, Jim, I'll do that."

They stood there physically aware of each other. She noticed how hard, tall, straight and lean his body was, not like those pasty-faced college boys she had to put up with, though a few of them weren't so bad.

She liked the fact that he was her age, too. It made things nice to have someone she could talk to, even though he was not on the same intellectual level as her college friends. He was simple and she knew she must be careful not to talk down to him. But then he had a wisdom all his own, learned from the harshness of the West. You couldn't get that from books.

Her grandfather had been angry when she had walked in on him out of the blue. He wanted her to go back East. He was afraid she would get hurt out here. This was a dangerous, unforgiving land that had no conscience. Only the strongest survived in the Nueces. She explained that to the young cowboy.

"Was thet what all the shoutin' was about?"

"I'm afraid so," she said. "Grandfather is worried I'll get hurt."

"Well, it looks like you won thet fight."

"Yes, thanks to you, Jim," she said. He liked the way she said his name.

They made idle talk for a few more minutes. She went up to the ranch house and he went to the bunkhouse. He expected to be greeted with a lot of kidding, some good-natured ribbing, but it never came. Instead they sat around him on their bunks looking serious.

"Look, kid," Mason said. "You know about the code, don't ya?"

"The code? Sure, I know about the code. What about it?"

"It's jest this, kid. Don't git too friendly with the boss's granddaughter. Things kin go bad, real bad and real quick. Ya get my drift?"

Blackwell nodded. He knew what Mason meant. Cowhands had a place and stayed in it. They didn't mess around with the boss's women or relatives. It was the code.

"I didn't ask fer it," the kid said. "It was Mr. Lamont's idea."

"Sure, kid, but he's expectin' you to follow the code. If ya can't do thet, well ya better ride out right now. If somethin' goes wrong between you and the girl, it'll fall all on you, not her. You git my drift?"

Blackwell saw the logic in Mason's warning.

"Yeah, I get it, boss."

"Good. Me an' the boys like you kid. Yer one of us now. We wouldn't like ta lose ya, right boys?"

They all agreed and patted Blackwell on the back, then walked back to their bunks.

"Goin' ta town with us?" Jakes asked the kid. "Give those painted ladies a whirl?"

"Sure," Blackwell said, but he didn't sound so enthusiastic about it. "I'll need a new mount."

"Take one of those outlaw horses we brought in," Mason said.

"Alright," the kid replied.

Half an hour later they all went down to the corral to saddle up and ride for town to have a good time.

Chapter 6

One morning a cowboy rode in from the west sector hunched over his saddle horn. He was pretty well shot up. Nate Lamont had the boys carry him upstairs to an empty bedroom. They all stood around the bed, staring.

"What happened, Tim?" Lamont asked.

The cowboy talked haltingly. "Well, Morrison and me was bringin' strays down to the brandin' site when we ran smack into a bunch of rustlers. They were pushin' about a thousand head."

"How many were they?"

"Maybe six. Coulda been more. Morrison is dead."

"What direction were they headed?"

"South towards Piedras Negras."

Alice Fuller came in with a basin of water and a cloth. She wiped the sweat from the cowboy's face.

"Thet you, Miss Alice?"

"Yes, Tim."

"Ya come back ta stay? I hope so."

"I came back just to see you, Tim. Just to see my favorite cowboy."

"Golly, Miss Alice." Tim tried to smile but couldn't. He sighed and the light went out of his eyes. Blood bubbled from the corner of his mouth. The young girl tried to choke back tears as she picked up the basin and left. In the hall she let go and started sobbing.

Nate Lamont was stone-faced. His eyes narrowed. The muscles in his jaws rippled as he clenched his teeth in anger. "Go get the bastards," he growled. "Give them a taste of Circle L justice, every last one of 'em."

"We will, sir," Clint Mason said.

They hurried downstairs to Lamont's den for extra boxes of rifle and gun ammunition.

"You want some extra men?" Lamont asked.

"No. We'll handle it," Mason said, waving a hand at Barns, Jakes, Sparks and Blackwell. "This is what we do best."

"Good luck, men," the rancher said.

They left the yard at a slow lope, heading for the west sector. It was a four-hour hard ride all the way.

"We'll never find them goin' this slow," the kid said. "Let's ride!"

"Hold it down, kid," Mason said. "You'll kill yer horse before we even git near 'em."

"But they're gettin' away, boss!"

"Not with a herd of cattle, they ain't. They can't do over twenty miles a day. Don't worry, we'll find 'em. Jest relax and enjoy the scenery."

Two hours later they stopped at a stream to water the horses and let them graze. They sat down, rolled cigarettes and smoked.

"Damn fine day fer hangin' a rustler," Sparks said.

"Yeah," Barns chuckled. "Jest the right amount a wind ta get 'em swingin' back an' forth. It sure is fun ta watch their eyes pop and foam a-dribblin' down their chins.

"Jesus," the kid said, "yer a bloodthirsty lot!"

In the afternoon they found Morrison's body. They dug a shallow grave, buried him with rocks on top.

"We'll give him a proper burying on the way back," Mason said.

They soon picked up the trail of the rustlers.

"They're headed southwest," Sparks said.

"How big a bite did they take?" Mason asked.

"I figure maybe two thousand head."

Mason nodded. Two thousand head. No, that was too big a bite. They couldn't let that happen.

"They'll know were comin'," Jakes said. "It's best if me and the kid scout ahead. We'll double back if we see any sign of them."

"Alright," Mason said in agreement.

Jakes and the kid rode off following the tracks left by the herd. They were an hour on the trail when the tracks got deeper and easier to follow.

"We're getting' close," Jakes whispered. "No loud talkin'. They might have a rear guard." Blackwell nodded.

A half hour later they came upon a straggler, a young calf with a fresh Circle L brand. Jakes cut a piece off the extra rope he had in his saddlebag and tied the calf to a scrub oak so it wouldn't drift off.

"The boys will find it and know we're close," Jakes said.

"Good idea," Blackwell said.

It wasn't long before they saw the back end of the herd half a mile away on a vast, open plain. The sun was low in the sky but Jakes was able to point out the riders.

"It don't look good," Blackwell said. "There's ten a them, at least!"

Jakes chuckled. "I was hopin' fer more. I'm in a killin' mood after seein' what they did ta Tim an' Morrison." He turned to stare into the kid's eyes. "You got a problem with thet, kid?"

Blackwell shook his head. "Don't worry, I got yer back, Jakes."

"An' I got yer back, too, kid," Jakes said.

The rustlers had most of the men at the rear of the herd, keeping an eye on the back trail. They carried their rifles up and ready.

"They're expectin' trouble," Blackwell said.

Jakes nodded. They stopped by some birch trees and waited. It wasn't long before Mason, Barns and Sparks came up. The big ramrod sat in his saddle looking on, watching the progress of the herd as it grew smaller in the distance. Suddenly he chuckled.

"What's so funny, boss?" Barns asked.

"They're the stupidest rustlers I ever seen."

"How's thet?" Sparks asked.

"We could stampede thet herd all ta hell an' back anytime we wanted ta. It ain't worth a quarter eagle ta them assholes."

"Let's do it, boss," Jakes said.

"No," Mason said. "Forget the herd. It's them sidewinders I want. An I swear ta God, I'll have their asses before this night is over."

"How ya gonna do thet, boss?" Blackwell asked.

Mason chuckled. "You'll see, kid, you'll see. Live an' learn, an' don't fergit what you see tonight."

"I don't git it, either, boss," Barns said.

Mason looked up at the sky. "It'll be dark soon. They'll stop ta make camp. They can't move the herd in the dark. It's too dangerous. Let's take a break."

They found a deep natural trench where they dismounted, unsaddled their horses and tossed their bed rolls. Barns made a small coffee fire and ate jerky and hardtack.

"What are we waiting for, boss?" Jakes asked.

"The moon. When it's high enough, we'll make our move. We'll need it ta do what we gotta do."

An hour later the moon was up. They packed their gear and checked the loads in their rifles and guns.

"You ever done this sort a thing before, kid?" Jakes asked Blackwell.

"Sure, lots a times, Jakes."

"Yer lyin', kid," Barns chuckled, "an' yer scared, jest like the rest of us."

That sort of relaxed them as they mounted up and followed Mason out of the trench. In an hour they found the herd. It wasn't moving now and there was enough moonlight to make out the four night guards. They were keeping the herd packed tight.

Mason stopped his men in the shadows of a stand of scrub oaks.

"Just what I wanted," Mason whispered. "Thet herd is ready to blow. They've got it packed too tight."

"Watch this, Blackwell," Jakes said. He slowly walked his horse to the back end of the herd, turned right and meandered lazily along the edge of the cows and right up to the rustler who was half asleep.

"That you, Butch?" the rustler asked.

There was a muted thud as Jakes slammed his Colt against the rustler's head and grabbed him as he fell to the ground. He brought the man and his horse back to where the others were waiting.

"Is he dead?" Mason asked.

"Yeah," Jakes said. "I busted his head in." He let the body slide slowly onto the grass and said to Blackwell, "An ol' Indian trick, kid."

"Did you see any sign of their camp?" Mason asked Jakes.

"No. It's too well hidden," Jakes said. "I didn't even see a flicker of light."

Mason nodded and said, "I wonder how far are we from the Rio Grande River?"

"About ten miles," Jakes replied. Why?"

"If they get the herd across, we're out of business. We can't touch them. If we're going to make a move, we have ta make it now. An' I mean now," Mason said.

"About their camp. It'll be close to the herd," Sparks said.

"That's right," Barns replied.

"Then there's only one thing left to do," Mason said.

"What's thet?" Blackwell asked.

"Stampede the herd," Mason replied. "Head it for the river and then turn it left, then left again. Git it spinning in a circle until it settles down."

"What good will thet do?" Blackwell asked. He had no idea what was going on.

"It'll catch them buzzards a-sleeping," Jakes said. "You ever had two thousand head a cattle tryin' ta crawl in bed with ya, kid? It don't feel good, thet's fer sure."

They all nodded.

"Alright," Mason said. "Let's show them what a real Texas stampede looks like!"

The big ramrod pulled his Winchester and the rest did the same.

"We'll ride over to the north side and start the stampede from there. Let it rip for about two miles, then turn it to the left twice, in the direction of Eagle Pass. Don't let it stop until they're tired an' worn out."

They nudged their mounts at a slow walk. Half an hour later they were lined up on the north side of the herd. It looked like a big, black carpet in the night.

Mason fired the first shot that started the stampede.

Jakes, Barns and Sparks opened up a second later, screaming and shouting like Indians. Moonlight sparkled off the horns as the cows began to move away from the source of the noise. Soon they were moving with urgency and the ground began to shake under thousands of pounding hooves. A deafening roar rose up into the night sky as the black carpet began to roll along, trampling everything in its path. The forward surge tore the earth apart, sending shrubs and scrub oaks flying into the air. A huge, dark cloud of dust blanketed the surging herd, trailing behind it like steam from a locomotive.

The moving mass was followed by an ear-bursting bellow of anger from the frightened animals.

Somewhere in the middle of this enormous mass, sparks were seen flying upward. Bits of burning wood followed as the herd obliterated the campsite, crushing it to dust. The rustlers' horses were caught up in the middle and swept away like driftwood on that wave of destruction, some climbing on the backs of the cows for safety.

There was gunfire as the outlaws tried to take out the cowboys. Two of them were smothered in cow horns and disappeared under the wave. The last one was shot by Mason.

Two miles away, a ribbon of sparkling water signaled the location of the Rio Grande River. The Circle L boys spread out along the west edge of the herd and kept firing. The herd began to wheel around on itself, forming an inwardly turning circle, gradually twisting itself into a tight knot, moving slower and slower until it was bunched too tight to move any further.

Finally, the herd stood there complaining at the Circle L cowboys.

"That was fun," Barns said.

"Everybody okay?" Mason asked. Everybody was. "We'll hold 'em until sunrise, then look for the bodies."

By sun up, the herd had spread itself out and was eating grass and drinking from a nearby stream that ran into the Rio Grande. Mason and the boys searched for the campsite. They found six trampled bodies. Two of the outlaws' horses lay crushed nearby.

"I was hopin' fer a hangin'," Jakes said solemnly, "but this is just as good. Dead is dead, anyway ya look at it."

They had breakfast and by noon had the herd moving east towards Circle L land with six outlaw horses and their gear. Mason came alongside Blackwell. "You okay, kid?"

"Sure, boss," Blackwell said.

On the way back, they stopped at Morrison's grave to give him a proper burial and a cross with his name on it. It read, "Ed Morrison, Age seventeen. A Circle L cowboy." Sparks read from the Bible before they left.

Blackwell wondered how old the youngest rustler was.

Chapter 7

They rode into the Circle L ranch yard three days later, hunched over their saddles, dead tired and coated with trail dust. Blackwell noticed three people standing on the porch watching them. Two of them were Alice and her grandfather, but the other was a young man.

He was perhaps a few years older than either Blackwell or Alice, and was smartly dressed in a fine tweed suit and city shoes. He wore no hat and his thick, brown, wavy hair was combed back on his head. He had a mustache and striking brown eyes. Altogether, he was a handsome fellow and cut a striking figure.

Blackwell learned later that he was Frederick Turner, an acquaintance of Alice's from New York City.

While Mason peeled off to report to Lamont, the others headed for the barn to tend to their mounts. The horses had earned a big bag of oats and a rubdown. Blackwell's outlaw horse had performed well. It was long-winded and strong.

What Blackwell had noticed on the porch was that the young man was holding Alice Fuller's hand, and this bothered him. It was as if she had forgotten all about him. This gave Blackwell a feeling of rejection, as if he had put his brand on her and now she was being over-branded by this handsome young man.

Blackwell suddenly saw this young man as competition. He knew it was stupid to think that way, but the notion grabbed him and wouldn't let go.

"Looks like Miss Alice has a beau," Blackwell muttered.

"He's been here before," Jakes said. "He's tryin' ta git ol' Lamont ta give him his blessin'. So far he hasn't got it."

Blackwell listened in anguish. Deep inside, he felt angry and disappointed toward Alice Fuller. The way they had looked at each other meant something to him but, evidently, not to her.

He silently cursed himself. What a fool he had been. Mason had warned him about it. Did he think he was important to her? A part of her life? He suddenly realized it had been all about the horse, anyway. Only the horse. They could never be more than friends and not even really friends. He was nothing but a hired she could order around as she saw fit.

A few days later, while Blackwell and Sparks were mending the corral fence, Mason approached them. Frederick Turner was with him. Blackwell got his first close look. Turner looked even more impressive up close. He was solidly built.

Mason took Blackwell aside, out of earshot, leaving Turner to watch Sparks work on the fence.

"Kid," the big ramrod said, "this city slicker is gettin' in old man Lamont's hair, an' the old man can't take it anymore. He wants me ta keep the greenhorn busy. Well, I ain't got the time fer it. So he's all yers ta play with."

"Me? What about her, can't she keep him busy?"

"Well, thet's what it's about. The idea is ta keep him away from her as much as possible. Ya git my drift, kid?"

Blackwell was angry at first, but on second thought he settled down. The competition was being delivered right into his hands. "What should I do with him? He can't ride an' he don't carry a gun. Hell, he's all city!"

"Not so loud!" Mason cautioned. He waited a moment. "Jest keep him busy as long as ya kin. As a favor fer me. I'll owe ya one. Okay?"

Blackwell glanced over at Turner for a moment. He sighed and nodded. "Okay, boss, sure. I'll give it a try."

Mason smiled big. He patted Blackwell on the shoulder and said, "He's all yers, kid!" The ramrod walked back up to the ranch house to tell Lamont he had fixed the problem.

Blackwell walked over to Turner and said, "Hi, I'm Jim Blackwell."

"Fred Turner. Glad to meet you, Blackwell."

Turner grabbed Blackwell's hand and shook it vigorously. Startled at the sudden familiarity, the kid pulled away. "Easy on the handshake, Turner," Blackwell chuckled.

"Oh? Why? It's a custom in the East."

"Well, out here it has a different meanin'. It's mostly ta seal a deal or make a promise."

"A promise? What kind of promise?"

Sparks was taking it all in with a smile but staying out of it.

"Well, like if we promise to be pards or cover each other's back."

Turner smiled but Blackwell felt he didn't understand.

"A 'pard'? Oh, yes," Turner chuckled. "I've read about that in the pulp magazines. I suppose I just made us pards, didn't I?"

Sparks stifled a chuckle. This guy was really dumb.

"It ain't thet easy, Turner," Blackwell said with half a smile. "We ain't even close ta bein' pards."

Turner looked disappointed.

Suddenly Blackwell felt a softening towards Turner. There was something of a lost little boy look about him, an inner sadness. He seemed eager to make friends and be accepted.

The kid looked Turner over. His city suit was okay, but he'd need a hat, a cowboy's wide-brimmed hat. The city shoes were alright since he wouldn't be doing any range work.

"Have you ever shot a gun or rode a horse, Turner?" Blackwell asked.

"No, sir, I have not, Mr. Blackwell."

"Would you like to learn?"

"Yes, I think I would."

"Then come with me," Blackwell said.

He led Turner down to the barn. Old Ben Lewis, the saddle mender, the man who took care of all the extra riding gear, had a small shop in a stall in the barn. Once a cowboy but now too hip-shot to ride, Lewis was a fine saddle repairman.

He gave Blackwell a saddle blanket, a saddle and a hackamore. "Let's go, Turner," the kid said.

They went outside and Blackwell hung the gear over the corral fence. He turned to Turner. "Go in there and stand by the fence and wait."

"What?" Turner looked a bit spooked.

Blackwell opened the corral gate and motioned for Turner to go in. The city boy hesitated then stepped inside the corral. He stood waiting for the next instructions.

"Now what?"

"Nothing. Jest stand there. Are ya scared?"

"Maybe. A little. Yes."

"Well, don't be. Relax. Nobody's gonna hurt ya."

"Alright."

Sparks had stopped work. He came over to look on.

"Ya tryin' ta kill him?" Sparks chuckled.

"If he listens, he'll be okay. If not, it was an accident."

"Well, I hope he don't git bit or stomped ta death. It'll be all on you, kid," Sparks said, then went back to work.

Blackwell closely watched the horses and their reaction to the intruder. A dun mustang pawed the ground, not liking Turner's smell. Some of the other horses, a mustang and a pinto, backed away into a far corner. Another mustang bellowed its disapproval.

Turner began to shake. "I don't feel too good, Blackwell."

"You're doing fine. Try ta relax."

After about ten minutes, a bay mustang gelding, one of the outlaws' horses from the hide-peelers, came slowly up to Turner and sniffed him up one side and down the other, then licked his face.

"What does he want?" Turner asked Blackwell, his voice trembling.

"He wants you, Turner. He's picked you."

Blackwell handed Turner the hackamore and instructed him how to slip it over the mustang's head. It took a while, but he finally got it on correctly.

"Now what?" Turned asked. He had stopped shaking now and was almost giddy.

"Lead him slowly out here."

Blackwell waited until Turner and the horse were at the gate, then opened it to let them through. They took the horse down to the barn where the kid had Turner feed it a bag of oats and brush it down. After that he had Turner water it at the trough. Then he showed the city boy how to properly cinch a saddle.

"Show him you love him," Blackwell said. "Hug him and rub his head. Kiss him, if ya want."

Turner did so. In return the big horse neighed and nuzzled him affectionately.

"He's your horse now."

"How can I tell him from the others?"

"By those brands on his rump. This big boy's been over-branded at least a dozen times.

"When can I ride him, Blackwell?"

"Tomorrow," Blackwell said. "It's too late now."

"I guess I can wait," Turner replied. He was plainly anxious to ride.

"Unsaddle him and put him back in the corral," the kid said.

He watched to make sure Turner went through the proper sequences. As he did so, he got a sudden inspiration. "Say, Turner," Blackwell asked, "how would ya like ta stay down in the bunkhouse with us lowly cowpokes?"

"Really? No fooling?"

"No foolin'," the kid said. He was laughing inside thinking about the look on Mason's face when he and the city slicker walked into the bunkhouse together.

It took a few minutes for the shock to pass when the kid brought Turner into the cowboy's sacred domain. After a couple shots of rotgut and some good-natured kidding, Turner became a sort of a pet mascot and things settled down.

In a week, Blackwell had Turner riding like a cowpoke.

Chapter 8

Blackwell began to like Turner more and more each day. The young, city-bred man took the bunkhouse teasing with good humor and showed he was willing to learn from the cowhands.

Once day Blackwell went to the barn to see Ben Lewis and got one of the rustlers' guns. It was an 1873 SAA Colt .45 caliber taken from one of the hide-peelers. It had an oiled belt and holster of blackened leather. Blackwell also found an abandoned cowboy hat in the bunkhouse. It was made of blackened leather with silver buttons around its brim.

He gave them to Turner, got a box of forty-fives and took him out for shooting lessons.

Alice and her grandfather watched from the porch, waving to them as they rode off. She knew Turner was doing this hoping to please Lamont, to change his mind about him. He was trying to remake his image from eastern dandy to a man of the West.

As for Turner, he quickly realized how heavy a loaded gun and a belt full of bullets weighed. It soon felt like he was carrying a sack of rocks around his hips. On the first day he was chafed raw. Mason gave him a jar of liniment to ease the pain.

"You'll git use ta it," Blackwell said.

Turner nodded and looked skeptical. "Oh, sure."

Blackwell found Turner to be a willing and uncomplaining pupil. He listened to directions and tried hard. After a week and five boxes of shells, he could hit a stump at thirty paces.

"Not bad," Blackwell said.

"Teach me the fast draw, Blackwell."

"Okay, I guess it's time fer thet."

Blackwell went over the basics, starting with the correct stance. Then came the correct wearing and tie-down of the holster and the smooth pulling and fanning of the hammer. The thumb work when only one hand was in play. In two weeks, Turner was hitting bottles and cans from twenty feet.

"What's the best killing range?" Turner wanted to know.

"It's different fer everybody. I feel comfortable at fifty feet. Even seventy-five. But for a fast draw, thirty feet's good."

Turner nodded with interest. "Is there a rule you go by?"

Blackwell gave that some thought, then chuckled. "Don't let yer man git too close. Hit him as far away as ya kin."

Turner stared at the young cowboy. "My God, Blackwell, how did you learn so much about guns at such a young age?"

"I grew up with horses an' guns. It's all I know."

"Well, I envy you," Turner said sincerely.

Blackwell looked at Turner. "Kin I ask ya a personal question, Turner?"

"Sure, Jim."

"What's between you and Miss Alice?"

"I intend to marry her someday."

"Does she love you?"

"She hasn't come right out and said it, but I think she does. I know her folks in New York. They like me a lot."

After that, the kid didn't ask any more questions.

On weekends, Alice packed a picnic, and she and Turner went riding alone to a shady place by a stream a few miles from the ranch house. Lamont seemed to be pleased with the change in the young city man.

"Nice work," Mason told Blackwell. "Lamont is happy as a bear in a honey pot. So is Miss Alice. An' so am I."

Blackwell didn't know what to say about that. He'd heard from Turner what he didn't want to hear.

He was jealous of Frederick Turner.

Chapter 9

Frederick Turner wasn't what he seemed to be. Although he was a young, handsome, well-mannered man of good tastes, he also had a hidden past. Born in Brooklyn, New York, he came from a broken family. His father was a convicted criminal and his mother was an alcoholic prostitute. Turner was raised in an orphanage in lower Manhattan. He ran away from the place when he was fifteen.

In the city, he fell in with a second-story man named Benny. Benny took a liking to Turner and showed him how to break into homes and crack safes. Turner caught on quickly and the two became partners in crime. They were very good at it and lived well, staying at fine hotels and going to the theatres and social events. Social events were nice places to spot victims and follow them home, or merely to rob them right there.

As New York City was a celebrity town, Benny and Turner sought out celebrity parties on the elite north side where a lot of the brownstones were. At one such party Turner saw a beautiful young girl that took his breath away. After mingling with the crowd and talking to half-drunk people, the slick-talking Turner found out all about her.

Her name was Alice Fuller. She lived in a fine brownstone in upper Manhattan. He also found out her father was a big-time estate lawyer named Frank Fuller and her mother was Mary Lamont Fuller, the daughter of a wealthy rancher in Texas.

In between robbing wealthy socialites in Manhattan and the surrounding area, Turner managed to become noticed by Alice Fuller. He followed her to the library and introduced himself over a book of sonnets by Lord Byron. He accidently bumped into her again at the park and the museum as well.

He was so polite and gentlemanly she finally accepted him as a suitor and friend. He sent her candy and flowers, as required. This got him a date or two, and she finally let him meet her parents. They liked him very much. Of all of Alice's suitors, he was highly rated amongst the top five.

One day, Benny took a train to Florida and never came back, leaving Turner on his own. Turner knew Benny was headed for Cuba to spend his ill-gotten wealth, and that was fine with Turner. Anyway, he had wanted to go it alone ever since meeting Alice Fuller. He had fallen madly in love with her, never realizing that, because of who he was, he could never be anything more than a friend.

When Turner learned that Alice had had a spat with her parents and had taken a train to Texas, he told her parents he would go and convince her to come back home to New York. They were terrified that she would be kidnapped by bandits, or worse, and said they would be grateful if he brought her back.

That was Turner's first trip to the Circle L ranch.

After a month, he was finally able to convince Alice to return to New York. Even her grandfather was happy to see her leave. The Nueces was no place for a city girl, what with all the rustling and killing happening on a daily basis. At the ranch house, the girl had seen the results of the constant brutality. She had treated and bound the wounds of many a Circle L cowboy that came in off the range wounded.

Over a period of two years, Alice Fuller had run away to the Circle L several times after having disagreements with her parents. She seemed to be drawn to the place, but didn't know why. Perhaps it was Nate Lamont's blood in her veins calling her home. Maybe she was meant to be there with her widowed grandfather. She loved him more than anyone in the world.

Turner always showed up to plead the case for her parents. After about a month of urging from her grandfather and Turner and letters from her parents, she would return to New York and reconcile with them.

As for Turner, things were getting hot for second-story men in New York City. People of Turner's occupation found it more and more dangerous on each job they pulled. After two close calls, he stood back to consider his options. He could go to Cuba to see Benny, or he could propose to Alice Fuller and see how that turned out. Anyway, he had nothing to lose.

The day Turner showed up at Alice Fuller's house to propose, he discovered that she had run off to Texas once more. At her parents' bidding, he took the first available train and went after her. He was there with her for a few days when a band of five weary, dusty cowboys came in after a week of chasing what Lamont had explained to him were outlaw rustlers.

The big ramrod, Mason, dismounted first and came up on the porch where Alice, Turner and Nathan Lamont were standing.

"We got 'em, sir," Mason had said. "Killed every last stinking one of 'em."

"Good. And the cattle?"

"We brought 'em all back. Two thousand head. We put 'em out on the north sector."

"Very good, Mason," Lamont had said. "And young Blackwell? Any problems with him?"

"Nope. He can handle himself in any situation, sir."

Lamont nodded his head. "I knew he was right for the Circle L. I knew it the first I saw him, by golly,"

"He's the real thing, boss, he sure is."

Turner had listened, mesmerized by the ramrod's story of stolen cattle. He wondered who this special cowboy named Blackwell was.

He'd like to meet him.

Chapter 10

Alice and her grandfather were in the kitchen alone. "Honey, you'd best take yer friend an' go back ta New York and git married," Nate Lamont said with concern. "His playing cowboy doesn't impress me one bit, and you kin tell him that."

Nate Lamont's words cut the girl deeply. "Don't you love me, Grandfather? Don't you want me here?" she said with emotion.

He looked tortured, conflicted. "Sure I do, baby," the rancher whined.

Her face tightened. "No, you don't! I can tell! I'm a bother to you!" Her voice was strained.

"Don't say thet, sweetheart," Lamont whined. "It's just that it's too dangerous for you here. I can't keep you safe."

"No! You hate me!" Alice cried and ran out onto the porch. She stood there crying while he paced the kitchen floor.

Viola, the woman Lamont hired to do all the household chores his wife used to do, came in through the back. She carried a big wicker basket of sheets just off the clothesline.

"You ain't payin' no mind ta her like ya should. Thet girl worships you, Nate. You best treat her better or you'll be sorry. She'll leave an' you'll never see her again."

Lamont sat down at the kitchen table and put his head in hands. He sighed. "I guess with all the ruckus around here I haven't been giving her the attention I should. I need my butt kicked."

"You sure do," Viola replied.

She put the basket down, walked over to the stove and poured Lamont a cup of coffee. He took a drink, listening as a horse rode off in the yard. For a second he wondered who it was but the pressures of the moment quickly pushed it out of his mind. Finally, the rancher went into his den to attend to some paperwork. The boys would be back soon and he hoped there was no more rustling and killing to report, at least for one day. It was a constant struggle against those unlawful forces.

It was an hour later when it struck him hard. That horse that he had heard riding out, who was it? And where was Alice? Lamont shot up from of his chair and rushed out onto the porch, looking all around.

"Alice!" the rancher yelled.

He waited and got no answer, so he rushed down to the corral. Immediately he realized that the big black mustang was not there. "Oh, dear God! What have I done?" Lamont groaned painfully.

He was in a complete panic as he looked about the yard and found it empty. The boys wouldn't be back for another hour or so. Lamont wrung his hands and walked in circles, cursing himself for being so blind. She had only wanted some attention and he hadn't even given her that.

Eventually, he realized there was nothing he could do at that point, so he calmed down. Maybe she would get it out of her system and come back feeling better. She would be fine. He would pay more attention to her from now on. In a week or so, Turner and Alice would go back East and he could breathe easy again. He walked back up on the porch and sat down to wait.

It wasn't long before he heard horses in the distance, and soon after that he saw the riders coming. Mason, Jakes, Barnes and Sparks rode in and dismounted. When the ramrod saw Lamont he knew something was wrong.

"What's tha matter, boss?" Mason asked. "Somethin' botherin' ya?"

"It's Alice. She's been gone all afternoon. She rode out in a huff. It'll be dark soon."

A look of concern came over Mason's face. "Which way was she headed?"

"I can't say."

Turner and Blackwell came riding in from the west. Mason told them about Alice.

"Gosh," Blackwell said, "thet sure ain't good. We gotta go out an' look fer her!"

"It'll be pitch black out there in half an hour," Mason said. "We'd be runnin' inta each other in the dark. There ain't enough moon out ta see by."

A helpless feeling came over the group. There wasn't a thing they could do.

"Build a fire!" Blackwell said. "Make a bonfire!"

Mason nodded. "Good thinking, kid. If she's lost, she'll see it. Let's hope that's all that has happened ta her."

In an hour they had a huge fire blazing in the middle of the yard.

"Heck," Jakes said, "they kin see thet all the way ta Denton, I bet!"

"Maybe even in Uvalde!" Barnes said.

A few minutes later they heard the sound of horses.

"It's me," someone yelled. "Lang Carson, Marshal of Denton." Moments later the marshal and six heavily armed men came riding in to the yard.

"Saw your fire," the marshal said. "Thought the house was up in flames. But I see it ain't."

Nate Lamont came slowly down off the porch. "What brings you out this night, Lang?" Lamont asked. "It must be somethin' big." Lamont already knew the men with Carson were a posse, but he wanted to hear the details.

"I got a wire from Somerville that Mingo Slade's gang robbed the bank there. They killed five people."

"That's out of your jurisdiction, ain't it, Carson?" Lamont asked.

"Yeah, but the marshal up there thinks they're coming straight across Circle L land, making their way to Jimenez."

"That's in Mexico, just over the Rio Grande," Mason said. "That means they'll pass within twenty miles of us ta get there."

"That's the way I see it, too," Marshal Carson said.

"You have only six men," Lamont observed. "That's not enough."

"Yeah. That's why I'm here. I'll need four of your men, at least. Five dollars a day, posse duty."

Lamont sighed and shook his head in resignation. "I suppose you'll take them anyway."

Mason spoke up. "Marshal, Mr. Lamont's granddaughter is out there somewhere, most likely lost."

"That the reason for the fire?"

"Yes."

"Okay, then, if you give me four men, I'll look for her, too. We'll start out at sunrise."

"Use my bunkhouse, Marshal," Lamont said. He and the marshal shook hands.

In three hours it was sunrise. After a quick cold breakfast, the marshal and his posse rode out.

Later, Jim Blackwell rode out alone. He had traveled three miles when Turner came riding up alongside him.

"We got ta find her, Turner," the young cowboy said. "If she runs inta thet Slade gang, it'll be bad news fer her. Really bad. They'll take her inta Mexico an' do awful things ta her."

Turner's face turned pale. He suddenly realized he loved Alice Fuller more than anything in the world, more than life itself. In his rotten, thieving existence, she had been a beacon of purity and goodness. He was ready to die defending her, if need be.

"You cowboys, you have a code, don't you?" Turner asked Blackwell.

"Yeah, we sure do."

"Tell me about it Blackwell, won't you?"

"Sure, pard," the kid said.

As they rode along, Blackwell explained the cowboy's code to Turner. Turner listened eagerly.

Chapter 11

Mingo Slade and his men rode out of Somerville with fifty thousand dollars leaving five townsfolk dead and several badly wounded. They were miles southwest by the time Marshal Sears got his posse together.

Before leaving on the chase, Marshal Sears wired Marshal Carson of Denton that the Slade gang would most likely be passing his way, heading for Jimenez, Mexico, and that he should intercept them, if possible. But he was wrong about that.

The wily outlaw was actually headed in the general direction of Eagle Pass. And the fastest way there was across the Circle L's east quadrant. Once there, he turned southwest and headed for Piedras Negras. From there he would continue along the Rio Escondita to his hideout in Zaragoza. The law couldn't touch him there.

Slade pretty much knew the lay of the land in and around Denton because he and his men had rustled Circle L cattle on and off for years on a regular basis. He knew the Circle L Ranch like the back of his hands.

Stealing cattle in small amounts was a low-yield profession. It was hard work with little to show for it in the end. Robbing banks, however, came with the reward of taking large amounts of ready cash. And there were no middle men to take a cut. Of course there was always a posse to be dealt with, so it was a choice of lifestyles between rustling cattle or robbing banks.

About forty miles south of Somerville, Slade and his men sighted Marshal Sears' posse heading their way. It appeared to be a dozen well-armed men. As of yet, the posse had not seen them.

"Let's look fer a spot ta ambush 'em," Slade said.

A mile away they saw a gully. Slade purposely led his men through it to make tracks. Once on the other side he split his men into two groups of four. They hid their horses well out of sight and took the high ground on each side of the gully. After that they waited.

Half an hour later the Somerville posse rode into the trap. They never had a chance. Slade's men poured lead into them. Only one of the group managed to escape badly shot up.

"Let 'em go," Slade said as one of his men got ready to make the chase. "He's full a lead and likely ta die, the poor bastard." He chuckled sadistically.

They quickly regrouped and rode southwest across Circle L land, heading for the Rio Grande River and Piedras Negras.

They stopped to make camp and ate by a stream about an hour before sundown. Slade was pleased. They had made good time, and by tomorrow they would be across the border into Mexico with fifty thousand American dollars. He and his men would live in luxury for a long time before they needed to make another raid on the American side. It would be easy. Cattle Banks were everywhere, waiting to be robbed. And Mingo Slade was good at that.

At sunrise one of the guards came in, leading a black mustang with a beautiful girl in the saddle. Slade and his men stared wide-eyed like wolves at a lamb, not believing their eyes.

"Who the hell are you and where the hell did you come from, girl?" Slade demanded.

"I'm Alice Lamont Fuller, sir, and you are on my grandfather's land. Are you rustlers?"

"Well, now, ain't she a sassy one?" Slade chuckled.

"I'll ask again, sir, are you rustlers?"

"Oh, I done thet lots a times, girly. Right now I'm in a different business," Slade said. He looked the girl up and down. "So, yer Lamont's gran'daughter, huh?"

"Yes, do you know him?"

"Sort of, wif him on my back trail, swingin' a noose at me," the outlaw replied. "Yeah, he'd sure like ta see me swingin' from a cottonwood, alright. He sure would."

"Can I go now, sir?" Alice asked. "My grandfather is looking for me. He has men all over trying to find me."

Slade scratched his chin and nodded. "Oh, he has, has he? I guess he's pretty worried, then."

"Yes, so I'd advise you to release me, sir."

"Please don't 'sir' me, girly. My name is Slade, Mingo Slade, an' I'm a bank robber and a rustler," the bloated outlaw boasted with a smile.

Suddenly Alice Fuller realized she was in bad spot. She grabbed the reins from her guard's hand and tried to turn the big mustang. It didn't happen. One of Slade's men grabbed her and pulled her to the ground.

"Let me go!" she yelled.

"I'm afraid you'll have ta come wif us, darlin'," Slade said. "In case we meet up with some of those men you talked about. Yer gonna be our ace in the hole, ya see."

Mingo Slade walked over to the black mustang and looked it over. "Nice bronc. Is it yers?"

"Yes," she said.

For the first time Alice Fuller saw what Slade looked like up close. He was a huge man, wide as a barn. His face, hidden under his sombrero, was disfigured from fights and the harsh elements that left his skin burnt brown by the sun and wind. His unruly, coal black hair hung down to his shoulder, almost hiding his small, black, button-shaped eyes that blazed under a large forehead.

A chill ran down her spine. The man looked evil.

Without a word, Slade grabbed the reins of the mustang and swung up into the saddle. Jabbing his spurs into the horse's barrel, he yanked the reins hard to get it turned around. "Move, ya son of a devil!" Slade yelled. The horse screamed in pain, its eyes bulging in rage. "I'll show ya who's boss!"

The horse bawled loudly and shot off between the trees, across the stream and toward a large field beyond. Slade's men watched and laughed as man and beast fought for control, getting farther and farther away.

"Looks like the boss got his hands full," one of the gang chuckled.

"I hope he breaks his damn neck," someone muttered. Oddly, no one rebuked him.

"Then he wouldn't be a-takin' a third cut of the money, would he?" another remarked. It seemed there was no honor among thieves.

"You hungry, lady?" an old outlaw asked her.

"Yes, I am, thank you."

The old outlaw got Alice a cup of coffee and a biscuit with bacon. She sat quietly eating and planning her escape.

Chapter 12

They had been riding since sunup. After making camp for the night, Turner seemed moody and bothered by something. He hadn't said a word for miles. Finally, he spoke. "Do you ever think about death, about dying? You must think about it a lot out here with all the killing going on."

"Not so much," Blackwell replied. "It's something ya git used to early on in life."

"That's strange," Turner said. "I'd think it was the other way around."

"Nope. When yer time comes, it comes. There ain't nothin' ya kin do about it."

"I guess that's the best way to look at it," Turner replied.

Blackwell was the first to see them, about fifty yards away, in the aspens. A man lay on the ground holding onto the black mustang's reins with one hand. The horse pulled against him but couldn't get free. Sometimes it dragged the man along on the ground, making him groan.

"Help me," the man pleaded, "my back is plumb busted."

Blackwell dismounted and walked slowly to the horse. He spoke soothingly, petting its neck and forehead. Once it calmed down he pried the man's fingers from the reins.

"What's your name, mister?" Blackwell asked with narrowed eyes.

"Sam. Sam North."

"Yer lyin'."

"No, no, I'm Sam North from Somerville."

"Where'd ya get thet horse?"

"It's mine. Always been mine! Please help me, sonny, my back is broken!" The man gasped in pain. "Oh, God!"

Blackwell knelt down alongside the man and smiled sympathetically. "Look, I know yer Mingo Slade. Ya kin play all the games ya want, but yer back's gone. So how do ya wanna do this? It's yer call."

"I ain't Slade, I tell ya!"

"Okay, fine. Have it yer way, mister," Blackwell said.

He stood up and stared down. Slade groaned. "For God's sake, help me!"

"I can't," Blackwell said. "Ya can't fix a busted back."

He turned and started to walk back to his horse when two shots rang out. Bullets whizzed past his right arm. Blackwell whirled around in a crouch, drawing his gun. He saw that Turner's gun was already out and smoking.

"He was about to shoot you in the back, Jim!" Turner's gun hand was shaking. "I had to do it."

Turner had just killed his first man and suddenly felt all giddy. A notorious outlaw lay dead and he felt good about it, about doing it for a reason, to save a friend's life. It all seemed so clear now, this law of the gun.

"Thanks, Turner," Blackwell said. "I guess I got a little careless. I'm surely glad you had my back. Guess I owe ya one, pard."

Suddenly Turner felt very good. He reloaded as Blackwell had taught him and put the gun back in its holster. The weight of it now felt good. The barrel was warm against his thigh and felt comforting. He looked at the man's twisted body for a moment, then turned away.

Blackwell went to the mustang and checked it over. It had deep cuts on its barrel where Slade had hammered it with his spurs. "It's okay, boy," he said as he ran his hands over the animal. The mustang seemed to like the familiar touch and nuzzled the young cowboy. Blackwell rubbed its neck and ears and spoke softly to it. When he turned around he saw Turner throwing up in the bushes. His face was pale.

"Sorry," Turner said.

"Nothin' ta be sorry about, Turner. I did the same when I shot my first man."

"You did?"

"I sure did. I heaved my guts out. But you'll feel better soon."

"Thanks."

"We'll, let's see how this plays out, Turner," Blackwell said.

They mounted up and rode slowly along, following Slade's back trail. The mustang followed on its own, and Turner came up behind. They soon rode into the trees and saw the camp of the outlaws a hundred yards away.

As they came closer, they saw Alice. An outlaw stood beside her with his gun to her head. Blackwell and Turner stopped.

"Are you okay, Alice?" Turner asked with concern.

"Yes, Frederick. A little roughed up, but okay."

"There's a posse comin' this way," Blackwell said. "They heard the shots back there. They'll be here in a half hour. Yer boss is dead."

"Yeah? Who says?" one of them asked.

"I do," Turner said, almost boasting. "I shot him."

The outlaws looked at each other for a moment. The one with the gun on Alice spoke. "So, what's the next move, then?"

"Who are you?" Blackwell asked.

"Turk Russell. Second gun."

"Kin we climb down an' talk?" Blackwell asked.

"You kin, but not him," Russell said, nodding at Turner.

Turner sat tense in his saddle, his hand by his gun, staring at Alice.

"Sure, jest me," Blackwell said as he slid slowly out of the saddle to face the outlaw called Russell.

"An' keep yer hands where we kin see 'em, friend. Or we'll have ta drill ya," Russell said.

Another outlaw stepped forward and said suspiciously, "I'd like it better if them two jest dropped their guns." He stared at Blackwell for a moment. A look of surprise came over his face. "Say, kid, ain't I seen you before?"

"Maybe," Blackwell replied. "You ever been around Sierra Blanca?"

A bolt of recognition hit the outlaw. "Well, I'll be damned! Yer the Sierra Blanca Kid, aincha?"

"Some people call me thet," Blackwell said. For a moment no one spoke. Blackwell looked at Alice. "Did they hurt you?"

"Not very much. They were just a little rough." She looked at Turner. "You shouldn't be here, Frederick."

"There's no place I'd rather be right now, Alice," Turner replied. Suddenly he was surprisingly calm.

"Look, Russell," Blackwell said. "You got the money. Take it and go. Leave the girl here."

"The girl goes, too," Russell replied. "She's our protection against the posse. They won't make a play as long as we got her."

The young cowboy sighed and shifted his weight on his feet. "Yer all gonna die here, Russell. Show some sense. Jest take the money and ride. Yer wastin' time jest standin' here an' talkin'."

Suddenly they heard horses in the distance. A few of the outlaws ran to the edge of the trees to stare out into the field.

"The kid's right, Turk! It's the posse! He's led them here!"

"Kill them!" someone yelled.

At that moment, Alice Lamont pulled away, exposing Russell's face and shoulder. Blackwell's hand was a blur as he dipped low and shot the outlaw between the eyes, knocking him flat on his back. Behind him, Turner, caught in the saddle, was fanning off shots, too, as best he could.

Blackwell felt the heat of bullets whizzing by as he fired again and again at anything that moved. The barking of guns tore through the trees and out into the field.

Suddenly Blackwell realized he had been grazed across his left temple, his left thigh and right side. His hammer was falling on spent shells and he was on his knees trying to reload.

Alice sat on the ground nearby, holding her side. Turner slid from his horse and sat on the ground, holding his stomach. Blackwell could see he had been shot four times. Suddenly it was very quiet except for the sound of crows returning to the trees.

After reloading, Blackwell crawled over to Turner and held him upright. Alice tried to stand but couldn't so she dragged herself over to them.

"Are you alright, Alice?" Turner muttered haltingly. His face was pale white and drenched in sweat. He had trouble breathing.

"I'm fine, Freddy," Alice said. She, too, looked pale and weak. She forced a smile. "You were very brave, Frederick. My grandfather would be very proud of you."

Turner tried to speak but only coughed up blood. "Yes, I was brave, wasn't I?" He paused to get his breath. "It's this place, this land, it does something to you, doesn't it?"

"Yes," she said, crying.

"Yes," Turner repeated after her. He said no more for a moment, then whispered up at her, "Alice, did I ever have a chance?"

Alice glanced quickly at Blackwell for a moment, as if seeking his help, then smiled down at Turner. "Yes, Freddy, you had a chance."

"I wasn't sure." Turner's voice was but a whisper.

"Well, I've always been sure about that, my friend."

"That means a lot to me now, Alice."

As he let out a big, long sigh, the light went out of Frederick Turner's eyes, but the smile stayed on his lips. Alice burst out sobbing. Blackwell lowered Turner's limp body down on the ground and stood up. Alice reached for his hand and he helped her to her feet.

"Hold me, Jim," she said and came into his arms. "I'm afraid, Jim. Hold me tight."

"It's alright, Miss Alice," Blackwell said as she came into his arms. He held her close, feeling the beat of her heart. "It's all over. They can't hurt you now."

"What about Freddy?"

Before Blackwell could answer, they heard the distant sound of horses.

Chapter 13

Marshal Carson and his men rode into the trees and saw the carnage. The entire Mingo Slade gang lay dead on the ground. Alice Fuller had two minor wounds, while Blackwell had three, none of them serious. Turner was dead and the money was recovered.

After the marshal had attended to Alice's and Blackwell's wounds, he had four of the Circle L cowhands escort them back to the ranch. Alice rode the black mustang.

"Tell Nate it's all over," the marshal said to Blackwell. "I'll take care of this mess."

"Alright, Marshal," Blackwell replied, anxious to leave.

They tied Turner's body on his horse and took him with them. No one spoke as they rode slowly along.

When they got to the ranch, Lamont came running out to meet them. He immediately had Viola take Alice up to her bedroom and sent a rider to Denton for Doc Stanford. The doctor arrived at the ranch a few hours later.

"How bad is it, Doc?" Nate Lamont asked.

The doctor sighed and shook his head. "It's more than bad. It's not the wounds so much as it is the experience. She's been through too much. It's done something to her. She'll be havin' nightmares."

"Did she tell you what happened out there?"

"No. She won't talk about it. I don't think she can. It's too painful for her to even think about."

"They said it was a bloody mess and she was right in the middle of it," Lamont said.

"Yes. It must have been horrible, all that killing, never mind the kidnapping part."

After the doctor left, Lamont went upstairs to see his granddaughter. "Are you alright, baby?"

She avoided the question and asked, "Did they tell you what happened out there?"

"Yes. Most of it, anyway."

"Where is Jim Blackwell?"

"In the bunkhouse. The doctor is looking at him now."

"He and Freddy saved me."

"Turner? He saved you?"

"Yes!" She starting crying again. "Oh, God, poor Freddy! They shot him so many times. It was like a nightmare. He was all bloody and bleeding. They were savages!"

The old rancher sat on the edge of the bed stroking her hand. "Don't cry, baby. It's all over now. You'll go back to New York and in time you'll forget what happened here. I'll take you back myself. You're in no condition to travel alone."

"But I won't stay there. I want to be with Jim Blackwell, Grandfather. I love him."

Lamont's face clouded over. Those were the very words he feared hearing.

"Look, my darling," Lamont tried to explain, "this Blackwell boy, well, he's just a passing fancy, my love. When you get back to New York amongst your friends you'll forget all about him. Nice boys from good families will come knocking at your door, dying to take you dancing and to parties. Don't you see? He's not for you, my sweet. He'll never be anything but a cowboy. He'll always be a cowboy and nothing more. It's what he is. That's all he is."

"I don't care. I love him."

"You don't understand, my dear. Do you know what a cowboy really is? What Blackwell really is?"

"What do you mean? What are you saying?" Alice said sharply. "What is he?"

"He's a killer. They're all killers, these cowboys. That's what it means to be a cowboy. They get drunk, sleep on the ground and kill each other. They're no good for anything other than killing and herding cattle."

"Oh, God, Grandfather! How could you say that? They saved your ranch. They died for you! How horrible for you to say that!"

"They get paid for doing what they'd do without getting paid. It's in their blood. Cows, horses and guns. That's their whole world, my love. Can't you see that? You said it yourself, they're savages. They can't live in the city. They would die without their cows, horses and guns. This is the only place they can stay alive."

He paused to see what effect his words were having on her. She just lay there staring blankly at him. He wondered if she were listening at all.

"Look," he said, "Cowboys are like flowers or trees that grow only in certain kinds of soil. If you plant them in the wrong soil, they wither up and die. Even watering them doesn't help. Do you understand what I'm saying, my love?"

Alice sighed deeply. She was tired and worn out. He had overwhelmed her with his logic. She couldn't find the words to refute them, so she began crying again.

Lamont patted his granddaughter's hand and smiled. He sat with her for a while, then left and walked down to the bunkhouse to see

Blackwell. He was sitting upon his bunk. The doctor had bandaged him up pretty well and he seemed okay. Mason was there, too, with Jakes, Barns and Sparks.

"How are you doing, son?" Lamont asked Blackwell. He didn't say it in a friendly way.

"I'm fine, sir," Blackwell said. "How is Miss Alice?"

"She's getting better. I'm taking her back to New York as soon as she is well enough to travel."

"When is she comin' back?" Sparks asked. He was secretly in love with her, as they all were.

"I don't know if she will be coming back, Sparks," Lamont said.

A hush fell over the group. They saw the intense look on the old man's face. He seemed burdened with a problem. Lamont looked around the bunkhouse and nodded to everyone.

"Men," he said. "I'm taking Alice home. Her mother and father are worried to death about her. She's in no condition to travel alone, so I'll go with her. But I'll be coming back and, when I do, I'll be making some changes at the Circle L."

Lamont gave Blackwell a sorrowful look. No one said a word so he turned to Mason. "Can I speak to you outside, Mason?"

"Sure, Mr. Lamont, sure."

Mason and Lamont walked out into the yard, far away enough where they couldn't be heard.

"I want Blackwell gone when I get back," Lamont said sharply.

"What was that, sir?" Mason wasn't sure he had heard right.

"I said, I want Jim Blackwell gone before I get back from New York. I'll give you his wages before I leave."

"Pardon me fer askin', sir, but why? He's our best man, sir. He's risked his life for the Circle L. We need him."

Lamont looked away for a moment, then back at Mason. "I don't care, get rid of him. I want him gone right after Alice and I leave. Is that clear?"

"Is it because of her getting too close to him? He ain't ta blame, boss."

"Don't question me, Mason. Just do what I tell you. Otherwise you can leave, too! All of you can leave, for that matter. Is that clear?"

Mason nodded. Lamont had changed. He seemed like he was mixed up and couldn't think straight. "Yes, sir. It's clear. Very clear."

"Good!" the rancher said harshly.

Mason didn't know this Lamont at all. He was cold and distant, almost a stranger.

Lamont walked away without another word. Mason watched him go into the house. He stood there feeling powerless. He didn't want to fire Blackwell and that stuck in his craw. Finally, he went back to the bunkhouse and spoke to the young cowboy.

"Yer done here, kid," Mason said. "Lamont wants you gone. Right after he leaves."

Blackstone shrugged. "Yeah, I figured he'd do it. After what happened between her an' me, he had no choice. He had to get rid of me."

"Whatta ya mean, kid?" Mason asked. "What happened between you two?"

"We got real close. But it wasn't me. I remembered what you said about the code. But she was in bad shape an' needed someone. She saw Turner git all shot to ribbons then watched him die, so she grabbed onto me an' I let it happen."

Sparks sighed. "Hell, if she'd a-grabbed onto me, I'd a-been happy as a bear in a honey pot."

"Yeah, me, too," Jakes said.

Barns said, "You're a lucky devil, Blackwell. I'd a-died jest ta please Miss Alice."

Mason said, "Yeah? Well, Turner became a cowboy jest ta please her, an' it killed him. The poor guy."

"An' he became a damn good one, too," Sparks said. "Ain't thet right, Blackwell?"

Blackwell nodded. "Yeah, he sure did."

"You think she'll ever come back here?" Sparks asked.

"Maybe, maybe not. There's no way of telling," Mason replied.

"Well, after what Blackwell here told us, she sure put him in a fix," Barns said.

"She didn't know," Blackwell replied. "Ya can't blame her. She was hurtin' somethin' awful. She wanted my help and I gave it to her."

"I reckon ya did," Barns replied.

"You love her, don't ya, kid?" Sparks asked.

Blackwell shrugged. "It don't matter if I do or not. I crossed the line. I can't blame nobody but myself."

Jakes sighed. "It looks more like she lassoed you and pulled you plumb over thet line, kid."

"No," Blackwell replied. "I let it happen. It wasn't her doin'."

After that no one said anything for a while.

Chapter 14

They buried Frederick Turner in a plot behind the bunkhouse reserved for the cowhands the same day they came back with the posse. It was a sad occasion as they gathered in his remembrance. On his headboard, they wrote:

FREDERICK TURNER

He Was A True Cowboy

Three days later, all the Circle L hands were gathered in the yard. One of the cowboys was waiting with a buckboard with luggage in the back. Nate Lamont finally came out with Alice Fuller. She looked much better. Her color was back and she seemed to be her old self again. She was wearing her city clothes.

She walked around the crowd saying farewell to each person. When she came to Blackwell she stopped and smiled up at him. "Well, Jim Blackwell, alias the Sierra Blanca Kid." She was her old self now. "I guess this is goodbye, I suppose." Her voice was unsteady.

"I reckon," Blackwell said softly.

She held her gloved hand up to be kissed. Instead, he shook it, smiling.

"I'll have to teach you some manners," Alice said.

"I guess so."

"Take good care of my horse."

"Sure."

She stared at him for a moment. He saw her eyes were moist, as if she was about to cry. Suddenly, she leaned in and kissed gently him on the mouth. Then, without warning, she forced a smile and playfully knocked his hat off, sending it flying away into the yard.

He went after it. By the time he got back, she was sitting beside Lamont on the buckboard, her back to everyone as it pulled away. They all stood quietly watching until it was out of sight.

Mason turned to Blackwell and give him his wages. The young cowboy shrugged and walked slowly into the bunkhouse to pack. Mason followed him. Walking up to the kid's bunk, he dropped down a wad of bills.

"What's thet fer?"

"The mustang. Lamont wants it for her. He wants you to leave it here so she can ride it, in case she gets the notion to come back."

Blackwell stared at the money for a moment. Was this Lamont's way of saying he wanted something of the kid's to remember him by? Blackwell was a legend at the Circle L ranch. Lamont would be telling stories about him long after he was gone. He would never see another rip-snorting, wild cowboy like Jim Blackwell, known as the Sierra Banca Kid. Not in his lifetime.

"Heck," Blackwell replied. "He can have Blackie fer free."

Blackwell said his goodbyes and carried his saddle and tack down to the corral. The black mustang came to greet him at the corral gate, whinnying at him.

"You belong to Miss Alice now, old pal," Blackwell said, choking up. He was on the verge of crying as he hugged the horse. "You treat her like a lady, now, ya hear?"

In fifteen minutes Blackwell had one of the outlaws' quarter horses saddled up and was riding through the gate of the Circle L, heading for Denton. The trackers, Mason, Barns, Jakes and Sparks, stood watching him until he was out of sight.

"Damn it, it ain't right," Sparks said. "Lamont is doin' thet kid wrong."

Mason nodded. "Yeah, an' I don't like it one bit."

Denton was about a couple hour's ride. Blackwell intended to go around it and swing west to Del Rio, but by the time he got there he had worked up a thirst, so he tied up at the Broken Bull Saloon and went in for a drink.

Tack, the barman, came over. He remembered Blackwell from before when the kid had shot a double eagle on the fly. "How'd it go at the Circle L, kid?"

"Fine."

"I guess you'll be drinking soda pop, like before, right?"

"Yep," Blackwell replied.

He laid down two bits, grabbed a pickled hardboiled egg and a piece of jerky from the jars on the counter and began eating. Tack opened a bottle of soda pop and put it on the bar in front of him. He drank half of it down in one pull.

"I sure missed thet," the kid said with a big chuckle.

A few minutes later there was the sound of horses pounding up the road. It came to a stop in front of the saloon. Footsteps echoed on the porch as several men came in and took their places alongside Blackwell at the bar.

He didn't bother to look to see who they were.

"I hear they call you the soda-pop kid," one of them said. Blackwell recognized the voice. He turned and smiled.

"I thought I'd seen the last of yer ugly faces."

"Not yet, kid. Sparks figured you might stop in town for a soda pop. Looks like he was right."

"So you all came here ta see me drink a soda pop?"

"Thet an' ta say a proper goodbye. Us an' you been through a hell of a lot together. We're gonna miss ya, kid."

"Yeah," Jakes said. "Keep in touch. Let us know where yer wranglin', okay?"

"Sure. Kin you read, Jakes?"

"Kin you write, kid?"

They both chuckled.

Mason ordered a round of rotgut. "Set 'em up, Tack, ol' pal!"

"I'm buyin'," Blackwell said and laid a double eagle on the bar.

"No, ya ain't, kid," Mason said. "It's on me."

Tack brought over a bottle of red eye and poured four drinks. Mason and the boys drank a toast to Blackwell.

"Where you headed, kid?" Mason asked.

"I haven't decided yet. I might head west for Del Rio."

Mason said, "Ya might wanna stop at Rock Springs on the way. It's west of here, about thirty miles or so."

Blackwell smiled and nodded. He looked at Mason and asked, "What's up at Rock Springs?"

"The Flyin' G. It's always hirin'. It's run by Al Gaston. Mention my name. I use ta ramrod the place."

"I just might do thet," Blackwell replied.

They finished their drinks and Mason and the rest all shook Blackwell's hand.

Mason said, "Well, see ya around, kid."

Mason, Barns, Jakes and Sparks went out the door. In a few moments Blackwell heard them ride away. He chuckled.

"What's so funny, Blackwell?" Tack asked.

"Nothin'," Blackwell replied.

In truth, he didn't really know why he laughed except that the whole thing seemed unreal. It had happened so fast. One day he was connected and grounded, and the next day he was cut loose to wander about like a lost calf.

He left the Broken Bull. Once on the porch, Blackwell stopped to look around for a moment then swung up into the saddle and headed west.

Outside of Denton he hit wide-open country. The road snaked off into the distance, disappearing on the horizon under a dome of blue sky and white clouds. Eagles wheeled high above on the currents. It was a fine day and he suddenly felt free for the first time in months. Blackwell let out a rebel yell and urged his mount into a run. The wind slapped the hat back on his head. A few miles down the road he slowed down to a lope.

That evening he camped out under the stars. By the middle of the afternoon the next day he rode into the yard of the Flying G Ranch. Blackwell mentioned Mason's name and was hired on the spot.

Chapter 15

Nate Lamont's late wife, Judith, had sent their only child, Mary, to New York for a formal education when the girl was eighteen years old. She wasn't going to have her daughter marry a cowboy. Besides, the Nueces was a wild and dangerous land.

Mary Lamont was twenty when she met and married New York lawyer Frank Fuller. A year later she had a baby girl named Alice.

When Alice Lamont Fuller reached the age of seventeen, she ran away to the Nueces to be with her grandfather. There was something inside her that drew her to that savage land in Texas. After letting her stay a while and teaching her how to ride and shoot, Nate sent her home again.

The following year, during summer college break, Alice was right back at the Circle L ranch riding alongside the man she loved and admired the most, her grandfather, Nate Lamont. Often, Alice usually stayed too long and her mother would wire Nate to send her home to New York to finish her education.

Sometimes they would send a young man named Frederick Turner to bring her back because she refused to leave. This seemed to work. Nate tolerated the city boy as long as he stayed out of the way.

When Nate Lamont took his granddaughter home to New York after her horrible experience with the outlaws, he met his only daughter, Mary, for the first time in almost forty years.

He suddenly realized three things. First, Mary was a stranger, and he, Nate Lamont was now an old man with a broken body, well into his late sixties. The third thing was, he didn't like the city.

It was all narrow trails boxed in by towering buildings that shut out the air and the sun. The sounds of one-horse carriages rattling on cobblestone streets went on night and day. The howl of the coyotes and timber wolves were replaced by meowing cats and barking dogs.

And worse than that, city folk walked too much. A cowboy never walked when he could ride, even if it was up the street. Any distance over fifty yards called for a ride.

Nate wanted to leave the day after his arrival, but was talked into staying a few more days. He agreed and then, the next day, it happened. While riding a cable car packed to the gills with people, old Nate Lamont's body shuddered. He gasped for air and collapsed with a heart attack.

Young Alice took it upon herself to care for her beloved grandfather and dedicated her time to making him well again. In a week, she had him on his feet and walking with a cane. The doctor had ordered him to take it easy. He also told Alice old Nate would never be the man he once was. Nate himself knew it. Something deep inside of him had broken and could never be fixed.

The second week in New York, Nate talked to Alice. "Remember what I told you a while back in the Nueces, baby?"

"About what, Grandfather?"

"About plantin' a tree in special soil?"

"Yes. It was about cowboys."

"Yes, about cowboys. Well, you can't plant me here, little darlin'. I have ta go back to the Circle L. It needs me and I need it. And that's how it is."

Alice nodded. Actually it was what she wanted to hear.

"Will you take me back home to the Circle L, honey?" old Nate asked.

"Yes, Grandfather, I'll take you back."

Old Nate Lamont stroked his granddaughter's face and smiled. "Alice, honey, yer a Nueces Lamont through and through, baby. Yer a Texas gal and always will be. You've got yer grandmother's blood in you."

"Thank you, Grandfather."

"An' now that I've seen the caliber of them college boys who come courting you, I do believe I was wrong about young Blackwell. They ain't half the man he is. They wouldn't last two days in the Nueces." Lamont paused a moment and stared into Alice's eyes. "Do you still love him, honey?"

"Yes, Grandfather, I still love him."

"Then let's go back there and hog tie and brand him, baby."

It suddenly occurred to Nate Lamont that Blackwell was no longer at the Circle L because he had ordered Mason to send him away.

Alice saw the look on his face. "What's the matter, Grandfather?"

"Nothing, honey," Lamont replied.

He decided not to tell her what he had done. He would figure it all out when they got back to the Nueces.

Chapter 16

The trip from New York to Denton was hard on Nate Lamont. He arrived at the train depot exhausted and weak. Arnold Fields, an old Circle L cowhand from way back, met them with a buckboard. He tried to help Lamont up on the bench but the old man got angry.

"I can do it myself, Arnold, darn it all! I ain't a cripple, ya know!"

Alice got up beside her grandfather and put a blanket over his legs. He held onto his cane for support. A few hours later they rode into the yard of the Circle L Ranch. Mason and his trackers were there to greet him. They were shocked by what they saw. The once invincible Nate Lamont had been brought down and laid low by his own body. He was now a broken man, a shadow of his old self.

Mason made the mistake of trying to help him down from the buckboard and was met with a blunt refusal. "Git away, Mason! I don't need help from anybody!"

"Sorry, boss," Mason replied and stepped aside.

They watched as Lamont struggle up the porch steps into the house with his cane. Alice stayed a moment to look around. "Where's Jim Blackwell?" she asked.

Mason looked uncomfortable. "Ah, didn't yer grandfather tell you, Miss Alice?"

"Tell me what?"

"He ordered me ta fire Blackwell the day you and him left for New York."

"What? My grandfather ordered you to fire Jim Blackwell?"

"Yes, ma'am."

"Where did he go? Do you have any idea?"

"Well, he said he was headed fer Del Rio."

"Del Rio? Where is Del Rio?"

"About a hundred miles west of Denton, ma'am."

Mason saw the devastated look on Alice's face. It dawned on him that it was never her idea to get rid of Blackwell. It had been Lamont's idea all along. Looking back on that fateful day, he saw how it had gone down. It was all the rancher's idea. Mason recalled the tears in Alice's eyes when she kissed Blackwell that morning in the yard, just before she got in the buckboard with her grandfather.

As Alice started walking towards the porch, Mason's voice stopped her. She didn't turn, but kept her face hidden. "What did you say, Mason?" her voice sounded low and strained.

"I said, if you want, we'll go look fer him, Miss Alice. Barnes, Jakes, Sparks and me. We'll go look fer him if you want."

For a moment she didn't answer, then she nodded her head. "Alright."

"We'll need some time, though."

"Take as much as you need."

"We'll leave in the morning, then."

"Thank you," Alice said.

As she walked up the porch steps Viola, the cook, met her and they went into the house together.

Mason and his men saw that Alice Lamont Fuller was no longer a foolish young girl. She was now a young woman and knew what she wanted.

Old Nate Lamont would need her. Alice Fuller was now strong enough to survive in the Nueces.

The next morning Mason, Jakes, Barns and Sparks headed into Denton and turned west in an attempt to track down Jim Blackwell.

Chapter 17

The Bull Horn Saloon was once a way station along the Rock Springs to Del Rio coach road. At the height of its day, it had been a lifeline in the cactus lands of the Nueces, an oasis in the middle of nowhere. Stagecoaches had stopped there to water their horses and give the passengers a chance to relieve themselves, get a bite to eat and stretch their legs before going on to Del Rio, twenty miles west.

When the road became too dangerous to travel because of the bandits, the stage line decided it wasn't worth the trouble and stopped using it. Anyway, people started to take the railroad trunk line that went in the same direction because a railroad car was more comfortable than a stage coach.

As a result, the waystation was taken over by an ex-outlaw who turned it into a saloon. It quickly became a popular hangout for criminals, cutthroats and riffraff. Unsuspecting travelers who stopped there usually met a sad fate. After being robbed and murdered, their bones usually ended up being bleached in the sun out behind the place. It was a place well known by the buzzards of the Nueces.

The Bull Horn Saloon was located about fifteen miles west of the huge Flying G spread, but none of the Flying G cowpokes were stupid enough to go there. They preferred the safety of the saloon in Rock Springs, a mile from the Flying G.

When young Jim Blackwell left Denton, he had stopped at the Flying G Ranch, as Mason had suggested, and was immediately hired to break horses for the remuda. It was the only job he was qualified for and luckily there was an opening. If there was one thing the kid was good at, it was handling horses.

Blackwell knew that a wild horse was a sensitive creature and it took an understanding hand to break one to the saddle. He had seen men break a horse using brute force and the result was that the horse literally went insane and tried to kill itself to escape the pressure. Blackwell came from a long line of wranglers and he had learned his trade from the best in the business.

That's why he ended up getting fired from the Flying G.

He had been at the Flying G for about a month when he caught Gaston's son beating a wild mustang with a whip. The kid walked up to him, grabbed the whip out of his hand and tossed it away. Gaston's son took a swing at

Blackwell and caught him good with a wild punch. Blackwell went down and the boy came at him and tried to stomp his head in with a boot.

Blackwell grabbed the kid's foot and kicked upward, catching him in the groin. He screamed for his daddy and fell on the ground, curled up like a baby. Gaston came running down to the breaking pen and grabbed his son up in his arms.

An hour later Blackwell was headed for Del Rio thinking he never should have listened to Mason in the first place. Another hour out and he saw the Bull Horn Saloon. He tied up and went in, wanting something to calm his anger down.

The place was packed. Blackwell ordered three shots of red eye. The barman, a big, hairy bear with the face of a bull, sneered at him.

"Sure, kid." The man's voice sounded like it came from below ground.

Blackwell nodded and dropped an eagle on the bar. The barman lined up three filthy shot glasses in front of him and poured them all full of whiskey. He grabbed the eagle up in a big paw and tossed it in the bar box.

"Drink up, kid."

And Blackwell did. He tossed the three shots down and slapped another eagle down on the bar. The grizzly bear filled the filthy glasses again and the kid tossed them down again.

After the sixth shot, things around the kid got a little fuzzy. A young girl materialized out of the cigarette smoke and put an arm around his neck and kissed him.

"Buy Thelma a drink, kid," the grizzly bear said.

"Sure." Blackwell bought Thelma a drink.

"Come on, handsome," Thelma purred. When she smiled the kid noticed she had a tooth missing in front. This made him laught.

Thelma led him over to a table where four men were playing poker.

"Here's a greener waitin' ta be plucked, Bob," she said. She pushed Blackwell down into a chair. Bob handed her two bits and she left.

"What's the game, Bob?" Blackwell heard someone ask. Seconds later he realized it was him.

"Deuces Wild, kid," he heard Bob say.

"Oh, that's a nice game."

One of the men at the table chuckled and said, "This kid is pickled, Bob. Let's jest take him out back."

"Sure," Blackwell said, "Let's take the kid out back." He giggled like a little girl.

Two of the men grabbed him by his arms and stood him up. He felt limp and weak, as if he'd been drugged.

"See what he's got, Len," Bob said to a third man.

Len started going through Blackwell's pockets while Bob watched. Len found a small wad of bills and dropped them on the table.

"Looks like he just got paid," Len said. He dug around some more and found some double eagles and put them on the table with the bills. "That's about everything, Bob."

"Take him out back. Put him to sleep," Bob said.

"I ain't tired," Blackwell heard himself say.

Bob laughed. "Sure you are, kid, sure you are."

A voice came from the shadows and said, "He said he ain't tired, Bob."

Bob stiffened and put his hand under the table to his gun.

"Who the hell are you?"

"I'm the kid's pal, Bob."

The two men holding Blackwell set him slowly down into his chair and turned around. The one called Len backed away from Blackwell. He stood next to Bob and dropped his hand down by his gun. He saw four men standing in the shadows a few feet away.

Blackwell giggled again and said, "Is thet you, Mason, you ol' sidewinder?" He slurred his words.

"Yeah, kid," Mason said as he kicked the chair out from under Blackwell, sending him sliding sideways across the floor out of the line of fire.

Guns roared from the shadows as Mason, Barns, Jakes and Sparks shifted and drew. Bob took a bullet in the chest. He fired off a wild shot that blew a hole in the table, sending splinters in all directions. The two men who had been holding Blackwell each got blasted in the stomach. They doubled over and fell face first on the floor. Len took a bullet in the heart just as he fired a wild shot that hit the oil lamp hanging from the ceiling above the table. Flaming oil spewed out of it and splattered on the table and floor. Flames burst upward as the dry wood ignited.

"Fire!" someone yelled. People started running for the front and back doors.

"Stand the kid up," Mason said. Barns and Jakes grabbed Blackwell's arms and stood him up. Mason scooped up the kid's money and stuffed it into a pocket of his jeans. "Okay, let's get the hell out of here."

They rushed for the front door, dragging Jim Blackwell like a sack of potatoes as the Bull Horn Saloon went up in flames.

Outside, the kid smiled and giggled once more. "Where's the dance?" he asked.

Chapter 18

Alice Fuller was down in the barn brushing the black mustang. She had just taken it out for a long ride across the fields, giving it a good workout. It pointed its ears forward as she spoke softly to it. "You miss him, too, don't you?" she whispered. "So do I. I treated him badly and I'm sorry. I just want to tell him how sorry I am."

It had been four days since Mason and the trackers had left, but it seemed like months. She wondered how the search was going, hoping desperately they would find Blackwell. Her thoughts were distracted by a distant noise out on the road. Her heart started to beat faster. She dropped the brush and ran out into the yard.

She didn't see him at first. He was lagging behind a bit. When she did, she started to cry. They all dismounted. Mason and his men walked down to the corral with the horses.

"Thank you, boys," she said.

"Don't hit him too hard, Miss Alice," Mason chuckled as he went by.

Blackwell stood staring at her from ten feet away.

"Ma'am, I'm lookin' fer a job," Blackwell said. "You got any use fer a worn-out cowpoke? I'll work cheap."

She ran hard at him. He caught her up in his arms and kissed her just as the black mustang came loping up out of the barn to scold him. It nuzzled them both.

"Mason told me about yer gran'pa, Miss Alice. How's he doin'?"

She wiped her eyes and laughed. "He's feeling better. But you can't call me Miss Alice anymore."

"Alright, then teach me what to call you."

"I will, when we're alone."

"I can't wait."

The black mustang nudged them again and snickered.

"Leave us alone," Blackwell said. "Go find yer own girl."

Alice laughed as she led Blackwell towards the porch steps. Halfway there he stopped.

"I need ta take a bath," he said. "I smell somethin' terrible."

"Later. My grandfather wants to see you, Jim. He has something important to tell you."

"Am I in trouble agin'?"

Alice laughed. "No, just the opposite. Come on, you'll see."

They went into the house.

The black mustang stood at the bottom of the porch steps whinnying for them to come out.

The End

Other western books by R. Annan

Western Stories

Fight for the Lazy M
The Red Bandana
The Salvation of Trace Logan
The Cowboy from Sierra Blanca

Jack Cordell Westerns

The Gunfighter in Winter
Long Ride to Hell's Kitchen
Owl Hawks
Gunfight at Barfield Springs
Shootout at Sanctuary City
Last Days of a Gunfighter

Clay Jared Westerns

Copperhead Moon
Cowboys of the Box R
Prisoners of Brimstone Pass
Range War in C Minor
Devil Wind
Showdown at Wamego Falls
Lightning Riders
Winter Kill
Gunfight at Wild River
Shootout at Rattlesnake Flats

About the Author

R. Annan is a well-traveled author with many interests. As a career serviceman, he served in Korea and Vietnam. He also completed a one-year course at the Defense Language Institute in Monterey, California, and graduated from the University of South Florida with a B.A. in Art and Art History. After taking a two-year course in screenwriting at the Hollywood Scriptwriting Institute, he established The Old Time Radio Club Time Machine as both a scriptwriter and an actor.

As a young boy growing up in the city, R. Annan never passed up a chance to see a western movie. His heroes were Buck Jones, Johnny Mack Brown, Wild Bill Elliot and John Wayne, to name a few. As an adult, he often wondered where his love of westerns came from. Perhaps it has something to do with his grandfather, John L. Annan, who was a cowboy from Helena, Montana, in days of old.

A Note from the Author

Thank you for reading my book. Would you please consider rating and reviewing it? I'd enjoy your feedback. Thank you!